Rocket to Limbo

"This is no ordinary star-jump: author Nourse has conceived a really credible plot with three-dimensional characters motivated by plausible reasoning. Furthermore, he has an almost uncanny ability to visualize the strange sensations and settings of the world of the future."

—*Kirkus*

"There is something haunting about ROCKET TO LIMBO . . . The author suggests that if man has faith, he can literally rearrange his environment to suit himself."

—*English Journal*

"The pace is good, suspense well sustained, and the conclusion satisfyingly surprising."

—*Best Sellers*

Ace Science Fiction Books by Alan E. Nourse

THE MERCY MEN
STAR SURGEON
ROCKET TO LIMBO
TROUBLE ON TITAN
(*coming in December*)

ROCKET TO LIMBO

ALAN E. NOURSE

ACE SCIENCE FICTION BOOKS
NEW YORK

ROCKET TO LIMBO

An Ace Science Fiction Book/published by arrangement with the author

PRINTING HISTORY
David McKay edition published 1957
Ace Double Novel edition published 1959
Ace Science Fiction edition/October 1986

Cover art by Don Dixon.

ISBN: 0-441-73339-5

Ace Science Fiction Books are published by
The Berkley Publishing Group,
200 Madison Avenue, New York, New York 10016.
PRINTED IN THE UNITED STATES OF AMERICA

To J. McP. H.

who will write his own some day

PROLOGUE

AD ASTRA, the words on the bronze plaque read.

The heavy metal sheet was bright and new, gleaming red-brown in the afternoon sunlight. Great bolts of brass buckled it to the base of the launching rack, a slab of gray granite cut in a single piece from the living rock of the mountains high above the rocket port. Reaching up from the rack, the Star Ship stood like a silvery needle, poised, graceful, eager to break away from the bonds of Earth—pointing upward toward the stars it sought.

To the stars.

The ship was named *Argonaut* in memory of that legendary ship and its crew that had plunged into unknown waters so many centuries before. She had been built with tireless care and devotion; years had been spent outfitting her for the brave journey she was now daring to make. The finest engineers on Earth had designed her to carry the growth tanks and fuel blocks, the oxygen and reprocessing equipment, the libraries and information banks that her crew would require during the long voyage. Her massive engines had been tested and retested to tolerances never before achieved on Earth.

They had to be, for these engines must not fail.

The ship's name was carved on the bronze plaque, and the names of the men and women of her crew. Below this the dates were written:

Launched: March 3, 2008
Returned:

There was no way of knowing when she would return, if she ever did return. There had never been a ship like the *Argonaut* before. This was no clumsy orbit-craft to carry colonists and miners to the outpost stations on Mars and Venus. The *Argonaut* was a Star Ship, designed for one purpose—to carry her crew across the black gulf of space between the stars. Her destination was Alpha Centauri; her voyage might take centuries to complete.

None of the crew who launched her would live to make landfall at her destination—they knew that. But their children, or perhaps their children's children might survive to send the ship blasting homeward again.

The *Argonaut* was bound on the Long Passage.

Up on the scaffolding surrounding the ship, lights were shining, men were moving quickly up and down as last-minute preparations were completed. The gantry crane crept up and down, up and down, loading aboard the final crates of supplies. For weeks the giant nuclear engines had been warming, preparing for the sudden demand of power to thrust the ship away from Earth's gravity. A chronometer clicked off the dwindling minutes. Gradually the scaffolding cleared of men; the crane at last came down and stayed, its lights blinking out.

High up on the hull a pressure door swung slowly shut, sealing the silvery skin of the great ship.

Around it, well beyond the range of blast gases, crowds of people stood waiting silently, thinking in their hearts what they could not put into words. Across the land eyes were turned upward, hoping to catch at least a glimpse of the ship as she streaked up through the quiet sky. Others saw it on silvery screens, or listened to the excited voice of the 3-V announcer. One thing was certain—the eyes of Earth were on the *Argonaut*, a crowded, war-weary, overpopulated, hungry Earth. The people knew the hope that lay behind the voyage: that the *Argonaut* would find a place where Earthmen could settle, could build homes and colonies, and so relieve the terrific press of people on their own crowded planet.

But there was another reason too for the voyage. The stars were a challenge that Man had to answer sometime. The time had come at last.

A young woman of twenty stood in the crowd, watching the ship with sad eyes. Her husband placed his arm around her shoulder and drew her closer to him.

"How are you doing?" he asked.

She shivered. "I'm scared."

"So am I. Everyone's scared, in a way. It means so much, and it's so frightening and yet so wonderful, too—you know?"

She nodded and clung closer. Her father was the first officer of the *Argonaut*. She knew she would never see him again, and she knew that he would never set foot on land again. The trip would take too long. His life was the ship now, and the ship was his life and responsibility, the ship and the children who would be born aboard it.

"John, I wish we could go along."

He patted her shoulder. "I know. I do too. But our work is here."

"A hundred years, maybe two hundred! How can they hope to make it?"

He watched the last of the ground-crew scurrying down the ramps, heard the expectant hush falling over the crowd. "I don't know, but they'll make it," he said firmly. "They will."

There was a restless stirring as the seconds passed. Then, like thunder gathering in the distance, rising louder and louder, the roar began. White flame blossomed from the jet of the ship, billowed out in a searing mushroom against the fallout dampers, as the roar echoed and re-echoed down the valley. Slowly, as if lifted gently on the magic fire the ship rose; slowly, then faster, higher and higher. The mushroom became a tongue of fire as the roar rose to a scream and the ship drove heavenward. The eyes of Earth followed the great finger of light into the sky, not daring to breathe, waiting, waiting—

And then the ship was gone. A sigh rippled through the crowds of people, and they turned their faces away from the sky. Slowly the crowd began to melt away, leaving the granite pedestal with the bronze plaque sitting in the gathering dusk, waiting to receive the ship when she returned. When? No one knew. No one there would live to see it.

The Long Passage had begun.

The young woman clenched her husband's hand, and without a word they turned away. She felt her child move within her, and she smiled.

He will be proud of his grandfather, she thought, if he's a he.

She did not know that the great-grandson of this unborn son of hers would be the man who would give mankind a Short Passage to the stars.

Silently, John and Mary Koenig turned and left the field as darkness gathered.

1

STAR SHIP GANYMEDE

AD ASTRA, the words on the bronze plaque read.

The block of granite that held the plaque was darkened with age; the bronze itself was green, the words obscure and hard to make out. Lars Heldrigsson shifted his Spacer's pack down from his broad shoulder and bent over, squinting to make out the letters.

Launched: March 3, 2008
Returned:

There was no date on the second line. Slowly the young man ran his eyes down the names of the crewmen and felt the old familiar prickle of wonder and excitement starting at the base of his spine. They must have been brave ones, those people, he thought. Trying to make a Star-jump with ordinary unassisted thrust engines! It seemed incredible, and yet they had done it. Where were they now? Dead long since, of course, but what about their grandchildren and great-grandchildren? Lars tried to imagine being born and raised in a Star Ship, depending upon tapes and films for knowledge of Earth and Earthmen left behind, never knowing the crunch of gravel under the feet, or the warm flush of a summer breeze on the cheek. Had they finally reached a landfall, ever, anywhere?

Certainly they had never returned to Earth. After three hundred and fifty years the granite launching rack still stood empty. The rocket port had grown up around it, engulfing it as the years passed, until it stood in the great central lobby of the busy Terminal, a silent monument to the desperation and bravery of the ship that was launched there.

Nor had the *Argonaut* ever reached the planets of Alpha Centauri, its intended destination, for modern Koenig-drive ships had searched those planets long and diligently and found no trace, no sign that Man had ever come there. All the near stars had been reached and explored by now—Altair and Vega, Alpha Centauri and Sirius and Arcturus and the rest—and nowhere had a sign been found. The *Argonaut* had become a legend, a brave gesture of the past, but the thought of that hopeless voyage never failed to stir Lars Heldrigsson, to make him eager to be off, impatient with the years of study that had been necessary to qualify him for the Colonial Service Patrol. It was a legend of greatness, and there was still a challenge in the stars that time and a changing world could never destroy.

Of this Lars Heldrigsson was very sure.

He shouldered his pack again, a tiny fifty-pound bundle, the weight limit allowed crewmen on Colonial Service ships, and walked quickly up the long ramp into the main

Terminal Concourse. He was large for his eighteen years, standing a full six feet two, broad shouldered, powerful. His height and weight had been something of an issue when he had entered the Colonial Service Academy five years before; since then he had gained another two inches, and barely passed the physical examination before graduation, not because of any sign of ill health but because of sheer size. His shock of yellow-white hair, his blue eyes and the flat, heavy features of his face revealed clearly his Nordic ancestry. He seemed to move slowly and ponderously. Throughout his life he had had to contend with smaller, faster ones who made the unfortunate mistake of assuming that Lars Heldrigsson couldn't move fast when he wanted to—to their enduring regret.

Now he stepped briskly out into the Concourse, felt himself picked up and carried by the streams of travelers, crewmen, colonists and Security men riding the rolling strips to and from the launching racks and loading platforms. Everywhere there was feverish activity and bustle. Across the way he saw lines of colonists waiting for their final physicals and baggage checks before boarding the Star Ships that would carry them out to new homes, rugged homes, perhaps, a far cry from the crowded mechanization of the cities of Earth, but homes where they could have land and food and a place to raise their children, homes linked to Earth by the strong bonds of Colonial Service ships that traveled to the stars and back in months.

And down the Concourse were the flashing lights of the shuttles leading out to the ships themselves.

Star Ship Tethys, now loading colonists and supplies for the fourth planet of Sirius, an old Colony, well established, rich in land, rich in Earth-mutated wheat, a sub-tropical paradise with room for many thousands of families to settle and grow, almost self-supporting now and soon to apply for independent elections and representation in the Colonial Council.

Star Ship Danton, taking men and machinery to the newly opened colony on Aldebaran III, a bitter place until Earth weather technicians and Earth civil engineers had carved a foothold for hungry Earthmen to find homes. A weather-beaten fisherman made his way onto the shuttle, with a gold ring in his ear and a tiny Arcturian monkey-bear on his shoulder, tossing three sparkling tele-dice in the air before him to amuse his pet and laughing as the creature batted at them with a tawny paw. There were great seas and many fish on Aldebaran III.

Star Ship Mercedes, exploratory to the far system of Morua, a double star with endless summer on its seventh planet, a good prospect for a new colony in ten more years, after the exploratory crews and the survey crews and the engineering crews and the pilot colonies had done their work in opening it; a new escape valve for Earthmen who no longer had room enough at home.

Star Ship Ganymede—

Lars felt his heart pounding as he stepped across to the rolling strip bearing the green and white cross of the *Ganymede*. His ship! The assignment he had dreamed of since his first day in the Academy—to ship aboard the *Ganymede* with Walter Fox, the man who had opened more planets to colonization than any man since the first Koenig-drive ship had left Earth; the man whose seal of approval on a planet was a virtual guarantee of a successful and healthy colony. This trip on the *Ganymede* would be no exploratory voyage, to be sure—a full week now before blastoff to bunk down the new members of the crew and get the Officers-in-Training settled in their duties; then a milk-run to Vega III to run a final check on a colony about to be opened to free colonization—but it would be a good trip to give an Officer-in-Training his space legs. There would be exploratories later, to unvisited stars, to unknown dangers. Time enough for that, Lars thought. Now it was enough just to be assigned aboard the *Ganymede*.

He glanced at the chrono on his wrist and stepped off the strip at a refresher booth. The assignment orders in his pocket instructed him to join his ship at 1400 hours; it was now only 1135. He had time to catch a shower and get himself into presentable uniform before going aboard. He wanted his first impression to be a good one. He could see himself in his mind's eye, stepping off the gantry into the entrance lock of the *Ganymede*, saluting the flag first, then the officer of the deck. Walter Fox himself, perhaps? No, that would be too much to hope for. But perhaps Mr. Lorry then, the second officer, returning his salute with casual briskness and saying, "Name, Officer?"

"Heldrigsson, sir. Officer-in-Training. Planetary ecology."

"Oh yes, one of the biology boys. You'll be working with Dr. Lambert, then."

"Yes, sir. That's what I'd hoped. Where will I find him, sir?"

"Up in the lab, I suppose. Glad to have you aboard, Officer." And another salute.

In the refresher booth skillful robot fingers helped Lars ease off his travel-stained uniform, picked through his pack for disposables and discarded them all with a whoosh down the disposal chute. As new clothing popped out of the slot Lars stepped into the shower stall, still glowing from his daydream. He relaxed as sheets of warm water and detergent sponges enveloped him. Even five years of intensive study and preparation at the Academy could never truly prepare a man for space—this was understood from the start—and neither could they explain in advance the feeling of tension and excitement, the indescribable fever of wonder and adventure that took possession of you the hour before you stepped aboard a Star Ship for your first Officer-in-Training assignment.

He had tried to explain it to Dad during the two-week graduation furlough from which he was just returning. It had been good to be home again for a few days, good to feel the warm winds coming up from the south, good to feel the bite of a pick once again in the rocky north-central Greenland soil. The farm was the same as he had remembered it, the heavy house built of glacial rock, the huge granite fireplace, the outbuildings, the fields of wheat spreading forth for miles in every direction. Dad had seemed unchanged, too, his face burned red and seamed by the wind, his hands rough and brown. Mom looked older and more tired, her eyes bright with worry as she greeted her son, but she had smiled through the worry, refusing to say a word to dampen his enthusiasm for his new assignment.

He had spent the first days with old Black, the huge Labrador who guarded the farm against all assailants, hiking the hills and valleys he remembered so well from his childhood. But he knew the question would come, and presently it did as he sat with Dad before the fire one night after dinner.

"Why do you want to go?" his father had asked him. "What are you looking for, Lars? What do you think you're going to find out there on a Star Ship that you won't find right here at home?"

Lars had grinned, a little embarrassed. Just like Dad, he thought, to dispense with preliminaries and speak his mind bluntly. "I don't know, for sure. I just know I've got to do it. I want to go where nobody ever went before. I want to do things that nobody else has ever done, or ever could do." He patted Black's massive head, felt the dog muzzle his hand affectionately. "Black knows why I want to go. Ask him why he always wants to see what the other side of a hill looks like."

"And you have to go on a Star Ship for this?" Dad lit his pipe and watched his son's face carefully. "You think all the frontiers are out there? You're wrong, son. Look at our farm, our Greenland. Why, in your Grandfather Heldrigsson's day our whole Greenland was an icecap!"

Lars shrugged. "The weather technicians—" he said.

"But isn't that a challenge? They took an icy wasteland here and made it the richest wheatland in the world. Look at the valley of the Amazon. It was a jungle once. Now its crops feed millions of people. Siberia, Antarctica—rich lands, son. There's work for you here on Earth."

The clatter of dishes in the kitchen had stopped, and Lars knew his mother was listening. He shook his head. "I've thought about it, and it's no good. This is your frontier, not mine. There's no more room on Earth, hasn't been for years. We need colonies, and the Star Ships have to find them. And I couldn't have a better ship than the *Ganymede*. You know that Commander Fox is the best planet-breaker in the business."

"It's a dangerous business."

Lars grinned. "Is that supposed to scare me off?"

"But you don't know how dangerous it may be," his mother said from the doorway. "Suppose you found aliens on some planet you went to, some race of horrible monsters."

Lars laughed and gave her a bear hug. "Now you're just digging up things to worry about. There aren't any monsters. Hundreds of ships have gone to hundreds of stars and never a monster. At least not an intelligent monster. They haven't found a single sign of alien intelligence anywhere. There aren't any aliens."

"Your Commander Fox thinks there are," his father said soberly.

"He's never found any. I don't think he ever will, either. It's just a pet idea of his."

"We still hate to see you go."

"You'd think I was going on a Long Passage or something," Lars said. "It isn't like that. With Koenig drive in our ship we'll be out to Vega III and back in two months. I won't be gone for so long."

And yet now, as he slipped into the factory-fresh uniform and checked his pack again, he felt a pang of regret at leaving the place where he was born and raised, where his family had lived since his great-grandfather had come north from Iceland to break the newly opened wheatland. It was a good home, and he would always love it, but he knew that his frontier, somehow, was on the other side of the hill.

Showered, and immaculate in the new uniform, Lars stopped at an Eating Bar for coffee and a burger-steak, offering his Colonial Service card to the robot cashier. Then he stepped onto the rolling strip again. His Service Card and order sheets were in his pocket, readily at hand. As he reached the loading gates, he noticed that no shuttle car was waiting at the end of the strip, which seemed strange. Usually a car waited at each gate to carry passengers out to the ships. He flashed his card briskly to the guard at the gate and started to push through the turnstile to the shuttle platform.

"Hold it, there!"

He stopped. The guard was staring at him suspiciously. "What's wrong?" Lars asked.

"You," said the guard. "Where do you think you're going?"

"To the *Ganymede*."

"The *Ganymede* is off limits to all personnel. That's straight from Security."

"But I'm on the crew of the *Ganymede*," Lars protested. "I can show you my orders."

Out of nowhere a gray-cloaked officer of the Security Police had appeared at Lars' side. "Trouble here?"

The guard nodded vigorously. "Caught this man trying to board the *Ganymede*. You know our special orders."

"Of course." The Security man turned his eyes to Lars. "You have papers?"

"Look, I *belong* on the *Ganymede*," Lars said hotly. "What's all the trouble?"

"If what you say is so, you have papers to prove it. Let me see them."

Lars fumbled open his order sheets and handed them over. The officer scanned them. "Sorry. This won't quite do. You'd better come along with me."

"But it says right there—"

"I can see what it says. I see a robotyped order sheet carrying a robotyped authorization to go aboard. But I don't see any countersignature."

Lars' jaw sagged and he felt his face flushing. "I—I forgot to get it. I was just starting my leave when the orders came, and it slipped my mind in the rush of things—"

The Officer gave him a peculiar look. "That so? You'd better come along with me."

Lars followed the Security man down a side corridor and into an elevator. Moments later they emerged into a long room one side of which was lined with cubicles. The officer stopped at a desk, flipped the switch on a viewscreen. "Hardy here," he said. "Get Jackson down here, and contact the *Ganymede* for me right away. We have a man here trying to crash the gate. May be carrying forged orders, we'll soon know. Yes, yes, of course it's urgent!"

He broke contact and turned to Lars. "Now, then. Let's see about those orders. In here."

He led Lars into a cubicle and strapped him into the seat of an Identi-robot. Lars pressed his palms against the charged metal plates, winced as the bright purple flash of the retinoscope clicked in his eyes. His card and orders were placed in a photochamber.

"I don't see why you're making all this fuss," he said. "Suppose I *weren't* authorized to go aboard the *Ganymede?* So what? Would it be such a crime?"

The officer just grunted and pulled the report sheet from the robot. "Okay," he said finally. "You just wait here a while." He went out, closing the cubicle door behind him.

Lars stared about the room, his puzzlement giving way to apprehension. What had gone wrong? Had there been a slip-up somewhere in the issuing of his orders? Certainly he had forgotten the countersignature from the port dispatching officer, but why should that bring Colonial Security Police down on him so swiftly? Surely there was nothing about the forthcoming voyage of the *Ganymede* that could interest Security so much—

Or was there?

He shook his head in confusion and settled down on the bench by the wall to wait.

He did not know how long he waited in the tiny, featureless room. His wrist chrono and pack had been removed before the Security man had closed the door. Lars rose and paced the room. He watched the current news-tape flickering on a screen in the corner for a moment or two, then snapped it off in disgust. Too many unanswered questions were crowding his mind for attention.

He knew that his position on the *Ganymede* had been obtained in the proper fashion, the same way all Officers-in-Training received their assignments. It was customary for each Star Ship to carry two fledgling officers, to prepare them by actual field experience for the duties they would soon assume in full on ships exploring, and opening new planets. The vast matching-plan system placed qualified men on the ships of their choice whenever there was an opening, unless the ship's commander objected. To most men leaving the Academy, the choice of ship was not important, but with Lars it had been different. He had set his heart on the *Ganymede*. When his appointment had come through he had hardly been able to maintain his joy.

But now something had gone wrong.

After what seemed like hours, footsteps stopped outside the door. He heard the Security officer's voice:

"You're quite certain of this now, Doctor?"

"Yes, yes, there's no question." It was a voice Lars had never heard, a deep and pleasant voice. "He belongs on the ship, all right."

"Well—if you're sure. I'm sorry we caused all the trouble."

"Nonsense. You couldn't afford to take a chance."

"No, we couldn't, considering the peculiar nature of—well, you understand."

"Perfectly. Now where are you keeping him?"

The door opened and the Security man came in, followed by a tall man of about thirty with sandy hair and hornrimmed glasses. "Looks like you're in luck," the Security man said to Lars. "I'll get your things."

When he had gone the sandy-haired man regarded Lars with a grin. "Boy, you picked the wrong time to go slipping up on little details like countersignatures! They'd liked to have had you breaking rocks on Titan for the next ten years. I imagine you'll be wanting these." He handed Lars his orders. They were now officially countersigned. "I'm Lambert, by the way. I think we'll be working together for a while."

"You're the ecologist on the *Ganymede?*"

"If you want to call it that. General biologist and jack-of-all-biological trades. You'll find that 'ecology' covers a multitude of sins on an exploratory ship. But we'll have time to break you in when you get settled a bit. We're leaving Earth tonight, you know."

"The shipping orders say next week!"

"Well! They do, now, don't they!" Dr. Lambert chuckled. "It's going to be a pretty short week."

"Look, I don't get this," Lars exploded. "First they nail me like a—a *spy* or something when I try to board my own ship, and now you tell me we're blasting a week ahead of schedule. What's going on? Why is Security so worried about the *Ganymede,* anyway?"

Lambert shot him a warning glance as the Security man returned with his pack and chrono. "I think we'd better get aboard before these boys change their minds. Let's go."

Moments later they were riding the gantry crane up the smooth side of the *Ganymede*. Lars clutched his countersigned orders tightly in an inner breast pocket. He could see the yellow light of the entrance lock above him, and felt again the surge of excitement in his chest. His ship! For the moment he forgot that his questions were still unanswered.

"You'll want to get bunked down first," Dr. Lambert was saying. "The other Officer-in-Training is already aboard, of course. You'll be bunkmates."

Lars nodded. "Who is he? Another bio man?"

"Navigator. I thought you knew." Lambert regarded Lars thoughtfully. "He's a classmate of yours, says you two are old pals. Though I must admit I didn't much like the way he said it."

"What did you say his name was?"

"Brigham," Lambert said. "Peter Brigham. Know him?"

Lars nodded slowly as the crane came to rest at the entrance lock.

Any ideas that he might have had that the voyage to Vega III would be a milk-run vanished from his mind with a groan.

He knew Peter Brigham, all right.

2

THE STRANGE CARGO

LARS HAD no opportunity to worry about his bunkmate when he stepped into the entrance lock of the *Ganymede*. Lambert spoke to the officer of the deck, a stout, ruddy-faced man whose up-turned eyebrows gave him an expression of continuous surprise. "Mr. Lorry, this is Heldrigsson, the other OIT."

"Your new whipping boy, huh?" Lorry nodded curtly to Lars. "All right, get him bunked in and see that he knows how to strap himself down. Skipper can't see him now anyway, so we'll have to wait until after blastoff."

They made their way below toward the bunkrooms. As they went they passed through the laboratories, narrow compartments lined with cabinets and technical equipment. Lars recognized the ultracentrifuge blocked in against the bulkhead, saw the tiers of incubators, the agitators and waterbaths, the cartons of pipettes and reagents still unopened, but secured tightly for blastoff.

"There's a big difference between routines you've learned in Earthside labs and the ones we use in the fields," Lambert was saying. "Here we have to be compact, but we also have to be fast, accurate and absolutely thorough while maintaining strict isolation technique. Let a foreign bug get loose on board a ship, and that ship may be dead. But we'll have time for the details later. Your bunkroom is aft of here. Better get settled now."

From far below in the ship engines were throbbing, sending a low, rhythmic vibration through every brace and floorplate. Lars stepped into the compact little bunkroom. It was hardly more than a cubbyhole, with two acceleration cots one above the other, two narrow wall lockers, and a two-foot walk space alongside.

Fortunately, Lars thought, not much time would be spent in quarters. A good part of his instruction had dealt with the organization of Star Ships and the pattern of life aboard them. He knew that this bunkroom, like all compartments on the ship, was sealed air-tight and pressure-tight when its oval hatch was dogged, setting in action the emergency oxygen supply. Beneath the lower cot pressure suits were stored, as well as a small sealed chest containing emergency food and water supplies. Disasters occurred on Star Ships despite all precautions; when they did, each separate region of the ship became a temporarily self-sustaining emergency unit for the men trapped there.

But under normal conditions the bunkrooms were used almost solely for sleeping, blastoff and landing. The Koenig drive did peculiar things to a man's insides, Lars had heard. According to the stories, you didn't care too much if the space was a little cramped. All you really wanted was a steady bunk to strap into, and nobody to bother you for a while.

A wall-speaker crackled and a metallic voice exploded in the tiny room:

"ALL HANDS CHECK BLASTOFF QUARTERS. BLASTOFF WILL BE ON SCHEDULE AT 2100 HOURS. REPEAT. ALL HANDS CHECK STATIONS."

Lars' heart began racing. In any Star Ship voyage the blastoff was a critical time. The Koenig drive could never be used safely until a ship had cleared a planet's gravitational pull. That meant that chemical and atomic engines had to lift the vast weight of the ship from the ground and thrust it outward with gathering speed until escape velocity was reached. Giant gyroscopes helped carry the burden of stabilizing and guiding the great ship's course through the first hazardous five thousand miles, but the spectre of disaster was ever present until the ship finally rode free of gravitational demands.

There had been ships whose gyros jammed and sent tons of metal and dozens of men plunging dizzily through the outer atmosphere into the sea. No one would forget the *Mercury,* which had struck New Chicago, jets still roaring, and rammed itself through four hundred feet of concrete and granite before the reaction chamber exploded.

But once in free fall the paramagnetic fields of the Koenig drive could be activated, hurling the ship forward through a distortion-pattern in normal space, carving the time of interstellar transport down to a fraction of that required with the Long Passage. The voyage to Vega III was scheduled for two months; it might take a day more, or two days less, but essentially only two months for a journey that would have consumed at least a hundred and fifty years on a Long Passage.

It was the Koenig drive that had given men the stars.

Lars began undoing his pack, storing his personal items in one of the wall lockers. That his bunkmate had already been here was abundantly clear. A used uniform had been thrown carelessly across the lower bunk; three shoes were scattered at random about the room, and both wall lockers had been appropriated. Lars sighed and began emptying the contents of one locker onto the bunk.

There was no question, he thought gloomily, that his bunkmate was Peter Brigham.

He had nearly finished when a voice behind him said, "Well! If it isn't the farmer boy."

Lars straightened up and turn slowly to the newcomer. "Hello, Peter," he said evenly. "It looks as though we're going to be bunkmates again, for a while."

"Just like old times, eh?" Peter Brigham lounged in the oval doorway, his gray eyes flickering over to Lars' belongings on the bunk. He looked older than Lars, though their ages were the same. He was of medium height, with jet black hair and a full lower lip that gave his face a petulant cast. But now he was smiling, a little half-smile that Lars had come to recognize the year they had bunked together at the Academy. "And here I thought you'd be up North trapping polar bears. I guess you made it through exams all right, after all."

"I made it. So did you, I see."

"Did you think I wouldn't?"

"Oh, no. I just haven't seen you since—you know."

"Mmm. The Prom, you mean." The dark-haired youth looked away. "No grudges, I trust."

Lars hesitated a fraction of a second. Then, "No, no grudges."

"That's good. Say, are you still lugging this around?" Peter held up the little pocket photo-file from Lars' pack, grinning maliciously. "Any new additions?"

"Yes. A new picture of the farm."

"How dull." Peter tossed it back on the bunk. "How are Greenland's icy mountains doing these days, anyway?"

"About the same as the New York jungle. You know, Peter, you ought to get out and plow a field sometime. It'd do you good. You might even get over this idea that the Northland is all cold."

"Well, I'll leave the plowing to you, I think." The half-smile returned. "I should really be up in the navigator's shack right now, but I thought here's poor old Heldrigsson stumbling aboard, and he'll need somebody to show him around." Peter's eyes narrowed. "By the way, I hear you had a little trouble coming aboard this man-trap."

Lars' muscles tightened. "A little bit. Why?"

"Oh, nothing. Just another one of the funny little things that are happening on this ship, that's all."

Lars went on unpacking without any comment. He had never liked this thin, bitter classmate of his, and he could think of no one he would less rather have as a bunkmate for two months in the cramped quarters of the Star Ship. But he particularly had no desire to confide his own conviction, just now crystallizing, that something was definitely not as it seemed on the *Star Ship Ganymede*. "It was just a mix-up," he said casually. "It was straightened out in a hurry."

"So I heard. Old Foxy went to bat for you. It's just as well he did, too. Those Security boys can get rough when there's something to get rough about."

Lars just looked at him and went on unpacking. For a while there was silence. Then as Lars unwrapped a spool of reader-tapes he had brought along, Peter's eyebrows went up.

"*Books,* already!" he exclaimed. "Aren't you sick of studying by now?"

"I've still got plenty to learn in my field," said Lars. *I suppose you have your navigation down cold,* he thought.

"Ah, yes. *Bugs of Other Planets and How They Bite.* But really, now, don't you get tired of all those smelly culture plates?"

"If it weren't for the culture plates, there wouldn't be any colonies," Lars said shortly. "Nor any live exploratory crews coming back, either."

"They'd never even get landed without a navigator."

"True enough, but the navigator doesn't give the go-ahead on a new colony site. Neither does the skipper. The exploratory crew can poke around all they like and decide anything they want to decide about a place, but when the chips are down it's the ecologist who says okay or no-kay. And he's got to know what he's doing."

"Well, maybe you're right," said Peter. "It's a pretty good field, I guess, for a plodder."

Lars flushed. He knew that he was slow. There were men like Peter Brigham in the Academy who could pick up their work quickly, with little or no effort. In five whole years Lars had never known Peter to thread a reader-tape until a week before examinations. But for Lars it was different. He had gotten through by slogging every inch of the way. He was a slow learner, a dogged worker who got through by digging and digging. Ideas came slowly to him; he needed time to tear through abstractions and foreign concepts to make them part of his knowledge. But once lodged in his mind, they were lodged for good. He wasn't fast, but he was stubborn, and he was thorough.

He only vaguely sensed that these two qualities alone had finally brought him through the Academy in the face of stiff competition from much quicker minds. In the Colonial Service there was a place for stubbornness and thoroughness that all the cleverness in the world could never fill.

Lars grinned suddenly. "Tell you what, you flit around with your star maps, and I'll plod, okay? But when we get to Vega III, I'll know everything there is to know about the place. I'll know what kinds of bacteria and viruses can wipe out this ship, and what ones we can use for defense. I'll know what we can use for food, and what we'd better keep away from. And I'll know whether there'll ever be a healthy colony of Earthmen on Vega III or not."

Peter looked up at him. "Is that what all those reader-tapes are about?"

"That's right."

"Well, I like to see you keeping busy," said Peter, "but it seems a little silly to me, considering the *Ganymede* isn't going to Vega III."

For a moment Lars thought he had heard wrong. "*What did you say?*"

"You heard me. We're not going to Vega III. We're not going anywhere remotely near it."

"But the dispatch bulletin—"

Peter snorted. "I know what the bulletin said. Routine run to Vega III for a final check on the new colony site. That's what's going out on all the news tapes, too, but it doesn't happen to be true. I've been keeping my eyes open, and if this ship goes to Vega III I'll eat those reader-tapes right off the spool."

"Where *do* you think we're going, then?"

"I don't know. I don't think anyone else on board does, either, except the skipper and the navigator, and they're not telling. The navigator gave me a three-hour lecture on Koenig drive navigation this afternoon while he was setting up the coordinates, but he didn't set them up for Vega or any place near Vega. He must have thought I didn't know *anything* about interstellar navigation."

"Maybe you don't," Lars said bluntly.

This hit a raw spot. "Look, he didn't even put the ship in the right Sector! I could assemble and disassemble this ship's navigation controls in my sleep, and I *know* those coordinates are fishy. But that's not all, by a long way. Why all the secrecy? Colonial Security has had this ship under constant surveillance for a week. They've got agents all over the place. Special ID checks on all the crewmen. They've practically locked us in here since we came aboard. Why all the precautions if this is just a routine run to Vega III?"

Lars shook his head. "Maybe they've uncovered a sabotage attempt or something."

"I doubt it. Nobody sabotages Colonial Service ships any more. And that wouldn't explain the other things. Like all those questions Commander Fox was asking."

"Questions?"

"About how we feel about the possibility of meeting up with intelligent aliens on some star system somewhere."

Lars felt a chill go through him. He had heard that this was Walter Fox's pet theme, that somewhere in the Universe intelligent aliens must exist, and that sometime, somewhere, men would encounter them. It was not a pleasant thought. There was enough danger and death to face in exploring unknown star systems without meeting hostile members of an alien race. It had taken the Colonial Service many years to quiet such fears, to convince colonists from Earth that there were no such aliens. And yet—

Peter grinned at him. "Shake you up a little?"

"It's nonsense," Lars snapped. "You're making a big case out of nothing at all."

"Oh, there's nothing glaring about it, just little things. And one thing I forgot to mention that isn't so little. The cargo we have aboard. It seems to be something very special, triple Security guard all the time it was being loaded.

Some of the crates were very small and very heavy—weighed tons. And one of them broke open on the gantry coming up. The Security boys covered it in a hurry, but I happened to get a quick look." The half smile formed on Peter's lips. "Whatever was inside was wrapped in a lead blanket six inches thick. Now, what do you suppose a Star Ship could be carrying that would require shielding like that?"

The wall-speaker interrupted them with a series of squawks and squeals. Then Mr. Lorry's voice flooded the compartment:

"All hands listen with care. The *SS Ganymede* will blast off in fifteen minutes. All hands strap down and wait for the broken signal. That will indicate the one-minute count-down. We will accelerate for one hundred and ten seconds on chemical thrust, then for seven minutes and twenty seconds on atomic thrust before the Koenig drive is activated. You will be uncomfortable, but this discomfort will pass. In each locker is a supply of amphetamine alkaloid to reduce the sensations of discomfort. You are advised to take two capsules now and a final capsule when the signal begins."

The speaker went dead with a click. Lars and Peter stared at each other for a moment. They knew what to do. Throughout Academy there had been blastoff drills, landing drills, and drills to cover almost any kind of in-space emergency. But now for an instant they stood rooted to the floor.

Then Lars was scrambling into the upper acceleration cot. Thickly padded straps closed around his arms, shoulders, hips and legs as he gulped the green capsules and waited, listening to the steady thrum-thrum-thrum of the idling motors far below.

It seemed like hours before the wall-speaker began a

broken signal in a slow monotonous rhythm. *Beep—beep—beep—* The lights flickered and went out, and still they waited.

Suddenly Lars realized that he was frightened. Sweat stood out on his forehead; every muscle in his body was tense. This was no jaunt to the Moon, no quick run to Mars or Titan. This was a Star-jump, the moment he had waited for since he was a little boy watching the flare of rockets rising from the southern sky. His mind was whirling with wonder and excitement. *To the stars,* he thought, and the thought echoed back in the darkness with a sharp chill of apprehension: *To what star?*

Vega?

Or somewhere else?

Suddenly the thrum-thrum-thrum rose in pitch, growing rapidly faster, louder. At first Lars thought he was suddenly sleepy as he sank back into the soft bunk padding. His body was heavy, his eyelids sagged, his face—But it wasn't sleep. A huge, unbearable feathery weight was pressing him down, crushing him, smothering him. He could hardly draw air into his lungs.

There was a shift, a jolt, as the pressure eased momentarily, then slammed him harder yet. *We're aloft,* he thought wildly. *On atomics now. Too late to go back.* He felt the powerful thrust of the engines driving through him until his whole body was vibrating with the ship.

Minutes passed. The pressure grew. He tried to move his head, but it was pressed with the terrible weight of acceleration against the headrest. *I can't breathe,* he thought. *How long—?*

Then, suddenly, the pressure was gone and a new sensation replaced it. He felt himself growing big, huge, mammoth as the room and bunk around him seemed to shrink away. He had a sensation of falling steeply, giddily away,

away from himself, away from everything. A rhythmic vibrato had begun, deep within his body and mind, growing faster, shaking him, frightening and deadly in its intensity. He tried to scream, but no sound came from his throat, only the silent vibration growing stronger every instant.

And then he knew what it was: the Koenig drive, thrusting the ship out into space with incredible speed, peeling light years away, shearing out beyond the bounds of light-speed and dimension, ramming the ship through a distortion of space itself.

To the stars—

They were aloft. Outside was nothingness. For two months their ship would be enclosed in a protective cocoon of energy, shielding them from forces beyond it that could wrench them into shapeless atoms. They were in space, en route at last.

As Lars sank back into the darkness of first-stage reaction to the drive, the thought drifted hazily through his mind. *To where? If not Vega, what star? For what purpose? With what strange cargo in the hold, wrapped snugly in six inch blankets of lead? What conceivable cargo—*

Vaguely the thought drifted from his grasp as he tried to find an answer, then slammed back sharply into focus. His eyes flew open and he stared into the darkness.

He knew the answer. There was only one thing the cargo could be. The ship was carrying bombs. Thermonuclear bombs, outlawed on Earth for centuries.

But *why?*

As he sank helplessly into sleep, no answer came to that question.

3

ROCKET TO LIMBO

HE WAS neither asleep nor awake. For eons it seemed that he lay still, enveloped in softness, yearning for sleep that did not quite come. The thunder and thrum of engines had taken on a musical quality, a militant beat repeated over and over and over like an ancient disc record caught in a groove.

Around him was blackness, impenetrable space blackness, but there were no stars, no planets. Muffled sounds came to him that he could not identify, and he felt waves of nausea passing through him. Then, with incredible suddenness the blackness was shattered by a piercing light as a first-magnitude star burst into violent flame, sending out streamers of color.

Lars opened his eyes, and the immensity of space collapsed around him, shrinking into the tiny bunk compartment, and the star became the wall light. John Lambert was standing by his bunk, swabbing his arm with alcohol.

"What—?"

"Just lie still and try to relax," Lambert said gently. "You'll be out of it."

Lars tried to sit up, but the straps held him down. "Out of it? Out of what?"

"Reaction, of course." Lambert swabbed his arm again and set the syringe aside. "Koenig drive sets up some very odd sensations, particularly if you've never been through it before. Feeling better now?"

Lars nodded dizzily and unstrapped himself. After a moment he slipped down to the deck.

Peter Brigham's bunk was empty.

"They needed him in the navigation shack, so I broke him loose first," Lambert said.

"How long—?"

"Seven hours or so. I checked half an hour ago and you were still out like a punch-drunk fighter."

Lars rubbed his forehead gingerly. "I feel like one, too. Does it always hit you like this?"

"More or less. You learn to modify it after a while. It's as much a psychological reaction as anything else. You're no longer legitimately a part of space-time as we normally know it. Just a kind of bubble slicing through it crosswise, you might say. Though the math boys would squirm if you put it that way. They've got a lot of fancy terms for the Koenig distortion field."

"I bet." Lars sank down on the bunk, still trying to orient himself. He felt as if he'd been sleeping for weeks. "Then we're on our way!"

"Yes, we very decidedly are on our way and then some. I would hate to have to bicycle home from here."

"But we're not on our way to Vega." It wasn't a question the way Lars said it. It was a statement.

Lambert stopped rewrapping the syringe and looked up, startled. Then he laughed. "What do you mean by that?"

"Just what I said."

"Somebody in your family a telep? Or are you just looking in your crystal ball?"

"I haven't been able to work tele-dice since I was six," Lars said doggedly. "You don't need to be a telepath to know that something is very strange about this little jaunt."

"Like what?"

Lars told him what Peter had said about the coordinates, about his own suspicions. He started to tell him what he had surmised about the cargo in the hold, but stopped. Something deep inside him seemed to be crying out, warning him. *Don't play all your cards at once.*

Lambert listened to him, and shook his head. "Sounds like you've done some fancy putting-together-of-two-and-two," he said finally. "And you're at least partly right, of course. The *Ganymede* isn't going to Vega III. But I don't know where she is going. All I know is that she blasted under secret orders, and that every high mucky-muck in the Colonial Service is nervous as a cat on a hot tin roof about her mission, whatever it is. This seems to be a very special-type trip."

"But they can't just shoot two dozen men out to nowhere without telling them where they're going!" Lars protested. "It's—it's against the law."

"You'll find that the Colonial Service does pretty much whatever it pleases, my boy, law or no law," Lambert said dryly. "What are you going to do about it? Protest? Whom are you going to protest to? You're in deep space."

"But Commander Fox—"

Lambert smiled. "I wouldn't go howling to Walter Fox

too quickly, if I were you. For one thing, he's called a meeting of the crew for an hour from now and may have some news for everybody then. Meanwhile, how would you like a glimpse at what deep space looks like?"

The starboard observation pit was in darkness when they entered. "We keep the opacifiers in operation in case anyone comes in unprepared," Lambert said. "Watch now!"

He pulled a switch and the pit was flooded with brilliant light. At first Lars thought it came from within the ship; then he saw that it was coming in through the huge observation dome as the opacifiers slid out of contact. Lars stared, his jaw dropping at the brilliant display that lay before him.

He had expected vast blackness, inky blackness studded with myraid brilliant pinpoints of light. He had taken training runs from Earth to the Moon on several occasions, runs made under chemical- and atomic-thrust engines alone, and at those times that was what deep space had looked like—huge, and empty, and lonely. That had been an awesome sight to see, the view of deep space that the earliest pioneers trying for the stars must have seen from year's end to year's end on the Long Passage.

But this was incredibly different, and incredibly awesome and beautiful. Running about the ship like a brilliant envelope a yard from the hull plates was a shimmering orange flow, flickering like tiny tongues of flame, surrounding the ship with fire. Beyond that there was no blackness, no sign of star-lights. Instead there were staggering flashes of brilliant light: orange, yellow, blue, violet, cutting impossibly complex patterns of color on the pale gray background. It was as though the ship were in the middle of a rapidly turning kaleidoscope, hanging poised in the shifting, whirling geometrical patterns, brilliant in their color, frightening in their intensity, in the very alienness of the impressions they made on the human eye.

Lars knew there was no alienness there, only a distortion of space and time, wrenched out of normal shape by the energy of the Koenig drive. What he was seeing was only the reflection of twisted, tortured energy-channels altered violently by the Koenig field. Not until the drive was finally shut off would the familiar pattern of black space and brilliant stars return to view. But then it would be a new star system, a new region of the galaxy with unfamiliar patterns of brightness to see.

He shut his eyes, dizzily. You could only watch for a few moments before the hypnotic luminosity became too dazzling. Lambert snapped the opacifier on again and activated the lights in the chamber. "Surprise you?"

Lars nodded, grinning sheepishly. "I didn't expect *that*."

"That's all right," Lambert said. "You're due for a few more surprises before this day-period is over, I think. Let's get down for that meeting."

It was an uneasy meeting.

Lars knew the moment he stepped into the small, compact lounge that he was by no means the only member of the crew who had sensed that everything was not right. The men were waiting in small groups, talking among themselves in low voices, casting sidelong glances at the forward hatchway leading to the control room section of the ship. Lars could see Peter Brigham across the room, talking rapidly to a thin, hungry-looking man with pale cheeks and prominent eyes, who blinked and nodded from time to time as he listened. Other men, coming past them, stopped to listen, bending nearer to Peter. From all the groups a hum of uneasiness arose, not angry, but not quite peaceful either.

Lambert raised his eyebrows, taking the room in at a glance, and Lars could see a shadow of worry cross his face.

They took seats near the rear of the room. "Your young friend seems to be doing a lot of talking," Lambert said.

"So it seems. Who's that he's talking to?"

"The skinny one? That's Jeff Salter. Assistant navigator. Morehouse over there is the navigator."

Lambert pointed to a cheerful-faced young man perspiring over a tape projector he was busy preparing for use.

"Films?"

"Looks like it," Lambert nodded. Another group of men came in and gradually settled in the bucket seats around the room. The lounge was well appointed for men with occasional lengthy periods of free time and very cramped living quarters. Tables tipped out from slotted storage racks along one wall; several cabinets were filled with playing cards and games. The far wall was packed with reader-tapes and several reading machines. In the corner a 3-V was flickering, poorly transmitted through the Koenig drive, but clearly discernible, a man and two girls building pyramids and spires with gaily colored teleblocks, teetering one unit up on top of another with a great show of difficulty as the structures built up crazily.

The forward hatchway opened and Tom Lorry, the startled-looking second officer came in, followed by a tall, heavily built man dressed in Colonial gray. Lars' heart jumped. It was the first time he had seen Commander Walter Fox, although the explorer's heavy features, severe jaw and shock of gray hair above pale blue eyes were as familiar to Lars as his own face in the mirror. Lars probably knew Walter Fox from tapes and films better than anyone on the ship did, for Lars had read every account of every expedition that Walter Fox had ever headed. Yet it was still a shock to see the man himself walk in, a commanding figure, firm and precise in his movements as he smiled and nodded to the men and sat down to the edge of a table in the front part of the room.

Not a man to tangle with, Lars thought to himself. Not a man to have angry at you, indeed, but a good man to have leading the ship any place the ship might be going.

Tom Lorry pounded on the table for order, and counted the men present. There were twenty-two, including Lars and Peter, a full complement for a first class explorer in the Colonial Service. Lorry nodded to Fox, and took a seat near the projector, handing a spool of tape to Morehouse. "Everyone's here, Commander."

"Fine, then we can begin." Fox looked slowly around the room, his eyes stopping for a fraction of a second as they met Lars' eyes, and again when they rested on Peter. "There's been a lot of talk going around the ship that there's something funny about this trip, that we've blasted under phoney orders, that we're not hitting Vega at all but someplace else, that we're heading for a plague spot someplace where we'll be quarantined for six months, and so on, and so on. So I think we'd better clear the air before we get into our normal intransit routines." He glanced at Lambert. "Anybody have any trouble with reaction this time, by the way?"

"Not to speak of," said Lambert.

"Fine." Fox leaned against the table. "These rumors are like any other rumors, they're false and they're true. It's perfectly true that the *Ganymede* has blasted under restricted orders, and that we are not bound for Vega." He paused to let that penetrate as a buzz of voices rose and the men shifted their feet uneasily. "Colonial Security regarded the secrecy as necessary, and I think you'll be able to see why in a minute if you'll let me go on. As for the rest of the wild stories I've been hearing bits of here and there, they're about as far off the mark as they can get. You men aren't very imaginative guessers. Let's have the tape, Paul."

Across the room Lars could see a malicious glint in Peter Brigham's eye as he leaned over to whisper in Jeff

Salter's ear. Then the lights dimmed and a wall screen sprang to life. The buzz of voices quieted.

The screen showed an image of a Colonial Service Star Ship, lying in its launching rack in Catskill Rocketport. At first Lars thought it was the *Ganymede*, but little structural details were different. Two gantries were busily loading the ship as Commander Fox's voice rose above the click of the projector.

"The ship you see here is the *Star Ship Planetfall*. She was a first class Colonial Service explorer, commissioned on November 17, 2347—that's just three and a half years ago. Anybody remember her?"

There was silence. Then someone said, "The *Planetfall*—yes! She was under Millar, wasn't she?"

"That's the one."

"Took her shakedown out to Sirus I and blew two generators?"

"That was before she was commissioned," Fox said. "It gave her a reputation as a jinx ship, but she was a good sound planet-breaker just the same. She carried the new modification Koenig engines that we have and a full exploratory crew of twenty-two men. With Millar aboard her, she was equipped to approach any planet of any star system that could be reached in the lifetime of a man, and to bring back all the data Colonial Service would ever need to open colony. You see her loading for a trip here. Good ship, the *Planetfall*."

They watched the flickering pictures in silence as the camera moved in close. Gantries rose and fell; all about the ship was an eager bustle of activity. The camera settled on crates of dry-stores being hoisted into the hold, ship's name and destination stenciled on the sides.

"Wait a minute—" one of the men said suddenly. "That ship was headed out into the Marakov Sector, wasn't it? A new star or something?"

"There's a man with a good memory," Commander Fox said. "Her first commission was for a big jump, out to the planetary system of a star known as Wolf. It's a long way out there. The near stars with familiar colonies are just around the corner in comparison. Wolf had been identified on photo plates, and that was as close as men had gotten to this star. We'd never had a ship anywhere near there before. But plate analysis said that it was a Sol-type star and that it had planets. *Planetfall's* job was to chart those planets and bring back all the information she could about colony prospects there. I don't need to tell you why. You know why Colonial exists. You know how desperately Earth needs new colonies for its people."

"I can remember the big hullaballoo when they blasted," a little man next to Lars said. "Full 3-V coverage and everything. They made a big production of it. That was just about three years ago, not even that long. But there was something I can't quite nail about it. When did she get back?"

"She didn't," said Commander Walter Fox.

There was silence in the room for the space of a long breath. Then a babble of voices arose. "But I heard—" "There was some kind of a report—" "Yes, yes! The Colonial Service said—"

"The Colonial Service damped it out cold," Fox cut in with a loud voice. "They made a brief report in certain of the official journals that the *Planetfall* had had a disaster in space—something wrong with her drive—and had been blown to atoms. They buried the story in the public press for all they were worth, and only a very few speculations ever met the public eye. They had to do it that way. They couldn't afford a scare breaking loose at home and wrecking the colonization program. But those reports had nothing even remotely to do with what really happened to the *Planetfall*."

The talking died as the Commander went on. "We know she blasted for Wolf two years and eight months ago. We know nothing happened to her drive because she was in drive-transmitted communication with the Colonial Service dispatcher on Earth from the moment she blasted on. She went into normal Koenig drive at the appointed time, and she reached the Wolf system. We know that. She reported six planets in orbit around a yellow-white sun, and she chose Wolf IV as the most promising of the six for a preliminary landing and pilot study. We know that, too, but that's all we know for sure. The *Planetfall* landed, and vanished. We had some signals from her during the landing process, then no signals." Fox snapped off the projector and raised the lights, then looked around at his crew. "Our commission is brief and to the point, gentlemen. We're going to Wolf IV, and we're going to find that ship if there's enough of her still in one piece to find. If there isn't, our job is to find out what happened to the pieces."

He leaned back against the table again. No one had anything to say. The men stared at him, and at each other, shaking their heads. "Well, that's about it," the Commander said. "Naturally, there will be some changes in the preparatory routines. From the standpoint of equipment and preparation, we're on a frank exploratory cruise to an unknown system. That means full study program when we arrive, not just the spot check you anticipated for Vega III. You'll have plenty of time to get ready, we'll be three and a half months en route. Now if there are no questions, we'll break this up."

The hungry-looking man called Jeff Salter had been whispering loudly with Peter Brigham across the room; now he bounded to his feet, a crease of anger across his forehead. "Wait a minute, Commander. We've got a question or two over here, I think."

Commander Fox frowned and faced the man. "All right, let's have them."

"Well, now, I mean this is pretty sudden, what with the men expecting a quick run to Vega and back." Jeff Salter rubbed his chin, frowning. "And I don't quite understand the story on this *Planetfall*. Did she make a landing on Wolf IV or not?"

"She landed, all right."

"There were messages that got through?"

"That's right."

"I see. But did she *crash?*"

Quite suddenly all attention was focussed on the tall, thin man asking the question. Beside him Peter Brigham was sitting, carefully staring at nothing. "I mean, if she crashed in landing, and the signal cut off, there wouldn't be much sense in sending a ship out to find her, would there?"

Commander Fox's frown deepened. "She didn't crash; at least the messages from her seemed to indicate a safe landing. There were some legible messages from her after she landed, but the atmospheric conditions apparently were terrible, and we didn't get very much. What we did get was all garbled and difficult to understand."

"But she didn't crash." Salter seemed to think about this for a moment, then, "What *did* happen to her?"

"That's exactly what we're commissioned to find out," Fox snapped. "It seems to me that you're just trying to make this hard to understand, Salter. You can read the orders as they came from the dispatcher if you want to."

"Oh, I'm not much worried about what the orders say," Salter said. "Thing that worries me is just what happened to the *Planetfall* after she landed on this place, and just what the Colonial Service is getting us into on this trip." He glanced quickly at Peter, then back at the Commander. "I don't understand all this secrecy, for one thing. Exploratory ships have cracked up before and there wasn't any fuss made about it—it was the breaks, that was all. So now why should Colonial Service be so almighty scared to tell the truth about the *Planetfall?* Why should they worry about how the colonists might react unless that crew found something on Wolf IV to be almighty afraid of."

"Let's keep our feet on the ground, shall we?" Fox's voice was suddenly angry. "What could they have found there?"

"That's what I'm asking you, Commander."

"We don't *know* what they found. I've told you that. We don't know what happened to them."

Next to Lars, Lambert was shaking his head. "Salter's just guessing," he whispered sharply. "Maybe their radio was wrecked, and surface conditions wiped them out before they could get it fixed. A thousand things could have happened. He's dreaming up spooks."

"He's not dreaming up anything by himself," Lars retorted. "Don't you see who he's been talking to?"

But Salter was on his feet again. "Commander, if this is just a simple reconnaissance run to try to locate a lost ship, and if all you know is what you're telling us here, the whole set-up looks mighty strange. Maybe there are some things you don't *know* for sure that you're very suspicious of and that we rightly ought to know about. Seems to me you've got a pretty good idea of what happened to the *Planetfall* when it landed on Wolf IV, and of what they found there. I think maybe you know why the Colonial Service was so scared of public reaction that they didn't dare publish the truth, too. Otherwise, why would we be carrying fusion bombs in the hold of this ship?"

Lars heard Lambert's breath hiss through his teeth. There was an electric silence as the men stared at Fox. The Commander's eyes turned for an instant to Tom Lorry, a glance of alarm, unmistakably clear. "Who told you *that,* Mr. Salter?"

Peter Brigham's voice broke out sharply. "I did. I saw them loading the things."

Fox rubbed his chin. He gave Jeff Salter a blistering glare, then turned to Peter. "Yes. I see. Maybe you're the one who should have been asking all the questions, Brigham. You seem to be doing my thinking for me. What does it all spell out to you?"

The answer was short and sharp in the quiet room. "Aliens," said Peter.

It struck Lars like a blow, and he felt something cold knot in his stomach. He stared first at Peter, standing defiantly across the room, then at the Commander. Suddenly all the strange things that had happened since he had stepped on the rolling strip to board the *Ganymede* twenty-four hours before fell into place, and he knew it was the only possible answer.

It was a fearful answer.

Commander Fox slammed his fist down on the desk and rose to his feet, his shoulders trembling. For a moment he glared at Peter; then he took a deep breath, his face gray. "All right, if you insist on the worst answers that might be possible, I'll give you the worst," he said harshly. "The ship is in grave danger. We have no way of actually *knowing,* for certain, any more than I've already told you: that the *Planetfall* landed, and lost radio contact, and never re-established contact. We couldn't get a clear picture of exactly what *did* happen from the messages. We could only guess, and suspect, and draw conclusions that might be wrong from what we did know. They ran into trouble—what kind of trouble, from what source, we do not know. But whatever they ran into, it stopped that ship cold in its tracks and it has never since been contacted."

Commander Fox walked back to the table. "That is why the Colonial Service has maintained such rigid secrecy; not because of what they knew, but because of what they *didn't* know. Those last messages have been studied and analyzed in every possible way, and only one conclusion seems to make any sense: that the crew of the *Planetfall* encountered a race of intelligent aliens on Wolf IV."

Not a word came from the crewmen now. They sat like stones as Commander Fox continued. "We're going to Wolf IV to search for that ship, gentlemen. We don't know what we're going to find there, perhaps nothing at all. Or we may be destroyed utterly the instant we land. We may face a hostile power with which we have no way to cope, or we may face a new era for Mankind in contact with a friendly alien race who can enrich us just as we can enrich them. But we don't know which, and from what we know of the *Planetfall,* we are forced to assume the worst. We're on an alien-hunt, gentlemen, a rocket to Limbo. And I am forced, against everything I believe, to carry the most devastating weapons Earth has at its command, and to use them, if necessary."

The Commander nodded to Mr. Lorry and turned to leave.

"If there are no further questions now, we'll fall out and get this ship into trim, I think. We're going to need it."

The men sat where they were for several seconds after the hatchway clanged shut behind the Commander. Then, silently, they arose and filed out toward their station assignments.

The talking didn't start until later.

4

"MUTINY COMES NEXT"

ALTHOUGH A casual observer would have noticed nothing at all remarkable, it was clear to Lars Heldrigsson that a fundamental change had come over the *Star Ship Ganymede* and her crew since Commander Fox had revealed the true nature of their voyage.

The change was certainly subtle. There was nothing definite that Lars could point to, nothing that could be pinned down in a report or dissected under a microscope, but it was there as surely as Lars himself was there. It pervaded the atmosphere of the place, haunting the dim corridors, whispering through the crew's quarters and lounges, invading even the quiet confines of the bio lab where Lars spent the greatest part of his time. There was a sense of uneasiness, of something building and growing, something of fear, something of violence, ever present yet never definable in any terms at all.

An old-timer would have said that the ship carried the mark of the *Argonaut,* and other old-timers would have known exactly what he meant even if they couldn't explain it to the youngsters. It was the mark of doom, of inevitable disaster that no human effort could hope to forestall, above all the mark of futility and hopelessness and fear.

Yet the *Ganymede* did not alter her course by any fraction. The thrum of the Koenig engines deep in her hold continued without faltering, driving her like a mindless juggernaut on and on. Her course was set and minutely adjusted; she responded to it with the perfection of the skillfully tuned machine that she was.

Lars' first reaction to the news of their destination was a baffling composite of excitement and fear. As he made his way from the lounge toward the bunkroom, his mind was flaming with excitement. So it wasn't to be a milk-run, after all! The prospect of a jaunt to Vega III and back, even considering his fledgling position on the ship, had never stimulated this sort of excitement. True, he was new to interstellar space; he had much to learn, how much he was only now beginning to grasp; even the simplest and most ungallant of voyages would have been endlessly new and stimulating. Even Peter Brigham as a bunkmate could not have detracted too much from that, he thought wryly. But Wolf IV was quite a different matter.

It was what the Colonial Service called a "new star"—unknown territory, a new sun to be seen, new planets to be explored; perhaps a new home for crowded mankind chiseled from the raw material of untouched ground. There were no preliminary reports to rely upon here, no records of previous exploratories. It was planet-breaking in the fullest sense, in a system never before seen by men.

But here his burgeoning excitement caught him up short, for he knew that it was not quite true.

Wolf the star and Wolf the fourth planet of the star Wolf *had* been seen by men. A ship had gone there before, and vanished. It had landed and disappeared without a murmur. What the *Planetfall* had met there no one knew for sure, but there was no way to avoid one simple fact: *they had met something*. And that was the source of the dread, a cold core of fear that Lars could feel deep in his chest and never quite put down.

Aliens.

There was nothing to think of, nothing to refer to, nothing even to fear but the idea itself. In Lars' mind the concept of alien life was a large gray cloud of nothing, bottomless and featureless. No one had ever contacted aliens before. Small animals and animated plants, yes, even insentient moving things that seemed at first glance to have minds of their own. But a sentient alien being, a thinking, intelligent alien creature, never. The thought was somehow awesome. The knowledge that such a creature might be waiting for them on Wolf IV was both fearful and unbelievable.

He wished, suddenly, that he could pretend that it was not true, and knew in the same instant that it was. It *must* be, for the *Planetfall* had vanished without a word.

Peter Brigham was in the bunkroom when Lars arrived. "Well!" he said maliciously. "I thought you'd be high-tailing it to the lab to study up on the biochemistry of unknown aliens. Or aren't there any tapes on that subject up there?"

"I was just on my way," said Lars.

Peter leaned back in the lower bunk, smiling. "Kind of puts a different color on the trip, it seems to me."

"How do you mean?"

"I mean we've been shanghaied, brother."

Lars groped for the meaning of the ancient word. Peter burst out laughing. "You know what it means. Back when they used sailing vessels on Earth, and took years to make simple two-hour voyages, they couldn't get crews to go willingly, so they got them drunk and sapped them over the head. When the men came around they were a little too far out to sea to swim home again."

"It's not the same thing at all," Lars protested.

"I'd like to see you get home from here on your own power. There's no difference, except that there are laws against this sort of thing, and they're enforced, and old Foxy has broken every one of them."

Lars regarded the dark-haired youth for a moment. "You seem mighty pleased about it."

"Me?" Peter grinned unpleasantly. "Not me. Why, I'm just as worked up about it as some of the others. Jeff Salter, for instance."

"Salter wouldn't have said a word if you hadn't fed him the questions, and you know it."

"All right, so what? Who's going to listen to an OIT on a Star Ship? And it was time *somebody* had wit enough to ask some questions. Or maybe you'd prefer to stand by and let Walter Fox butcher the lot of us, eh?"

"Why blame Commander Fox? He's acting under orders just the way we are."

"Sure. So was Millar of the *Planetfall*. Only the *Planetfall* didn't have quite the right orders to cover the situation." Peter started for the hatchway. "After all, the Colonial Service isn't a military organization. Every one of us signed contracts for this voyage, and the contract I signed didn't say anything about Wolf IV in it, orders or no orders."

Lars chuckled. "What do you think you're going to do?

Ask the Commander to please turn the ship around and go home again?"

Peter wasn't smiling any more. "You just keep your eyes open," he said slowly. "Old Foxy isn't quite through answering questions yet."

Then he was gone, leaving Lars staring at the clanging hatch. He stared for a moment. Then he roused himself and started for the lab.

There was work to be done.

Until his first hour in the bio lab with John Lambert, Lars had had no conception of the amount and variety of preparation required by an exploratory run to a new star. And after his first hour he had no time to worry about Peter or the crew or the ship's destination or anything else. As Lambert pointed out first off, there was more work to be done than any two mortal humans could hope to accomplish in the time they had.

So they set about to do it.

Much of it was chore and drudge work, but it had to be done. Culture media had to be prepared fresh, sterilized, poured into plates and stored. Glassware and instruments had to be minutely calibrated. Fresh reagent solutions had to be prepared with painstaking care, for success or failure of a mission could depend upon a fraction of a pH point, a quarter of a cc miscalculated. Lars spent hours at the micro-balances, weighing, measuring, dissolving, distilling, checking volumetric variations and molarity constants.

But there was other work, which Lambert alone could teach Lars. There were tapes to be studied, but in the field, when all the chips are down, only a man experienced in the fieldwork can teach. And Lambert was an excellent teacher. Where he might have been impatient, he was tolerant; where he might have skimped, he refused to. "You can't know too much in advance," he would say over and over. "On a new planet the crew depends on you for their lives. You have to know what to look for, what to guard against."

"But if it's a new planet, how can you know that?" Lars protested wearily. "I should think you'd have to wait and see."

"If you counted on that approach, your first trip would very likely be your last one," Lambert chuckled. "Naturally, we can't predict specific problems and dangers until we get there, but we can be prepared to meet broad classes of trouble. What about bacteria and viruses? We can be prepared to nail them quickly, find out which ones are dangerous, and prepare vaccines. What about the atmosphere? We can be ready to test it in ten minutes and *know* whether it can support us or not. What about plant proteins, animal proteins, the growing quality of the soil?" He slipped off his glasses and ran a hand through his sandy hair. "All we're trying to do is reduce the odds against us. You'll get on to it, but it means digging and digging."

And digging was what they did. As days passed Lars seldom left the lab except for meals and sleep periods. Doggedly he worked to learn the testing techniques, the analyses, the evaluation procedures. He studied the standard flow-sheet of procedure to be followed, and worked out with Lambert places where their situation differed from standard, special trouble spots, special problems. Lambert set up test problems, based entirely on speculation, then patiently went over them with Lars, pointing out a critical omission here, sure death to the crew there, and slowly Lars learned.

Yet he never could throw off the sense of dread, of growing danger as the ship moved implacably toward its destination. At the end was Wolf IV, and then—

What? What then?

At the beginning of the fourth day-period after the meeting in the lounge, Lambert was gone when Lars reached the lab. A few moments later he came in, puffing on his dead pipe, a worried frown wrinkling his forehead. He went about the lab grumbling under his breath until Lars said, "What's the trouble?"

"I don't know." Lambert shook his head disgustedly and sank down in a bucket chair. "There's something going on around this ship, and I don't like it a bit."

Lars put down the slide he had been examining and looked up sharply. "Going on? What?"

"I don't know. Nothing I can put my finger on. Maybe it's nothing at all, but no, by Jupiter, it's not!" He looked up at Lars angrily. "*Talk*. Grumbling and griping. Whispers. I know, put twenty-two men together in close quarters for a few weeks and there'll always be griping, but this is different. It's got an ugly tone to it."

Lars chewed his lip for a moment. "There's something I've been wanting to ask you."

"Shoot."

"Did you know all along we were going to Wolf IV?"

Lambert looked startled. "Not by a long way! I knew we were under restricted orders, all right, but I didn't know why! And I didn't know we were carrying fusion bombs."

"And yet you, of all men on the ship, should have known, it seems to me. I still don't understand the secrecy."

"They were afraid of leaks."

"So the news leaked. So what?"

Lambert looked at Lars narrowly. "Do you have any idea of the reaction home on Earth if news got out that a hostile alien had been contacted by an Earth ship?"

"Well—I—I suppose it would scare people a little."

"*Scare* them! My boy, you'd have a panic on your hands like Earth hasn't seen in centuries! Your colonization program would go up in one big puff of pink smoke. The Colonial Service would be legislated out of existence. Earth would start arming for very dear life, and God alone knows what would become of the colonies already established. The whole system would crumble, and we'd be back where we started three hundred years ago. That's what would happen."

"But why? If nobody has seen an alien, why be so deathly afraid of it?"

"That's exactly why." Lambert sighed and tried to light his pipe again. "Human beings are pretty brave creatures, as long as they know what they're dealing with. But put them up against something completely unknown, utterly inconceivable to them, and they'll panic. It doesn't make sense, but it's happened over and over. Fear of the unknown. It's plagued mankind since the year one, and we still aren't rid of it."

Lars blinked at him, and shook his head. "Certainly *everybody* wouldn't lose his head."

"Enough would to make it disastrous."

"But suppose the alien wasn't hostile at all. Suppose it was friendly."

Lambert smiled wearily. "Aliens, by definition, are hostile. Walter Fox has been fighting that idea as long as he's been in space. It's common sense that somewhere, sometime, in centuries of exploration, men are going to encounter an alien race in the stars. The aliens might be good, or bad. It would be a fearful gamble to find out which, but if they were good, we could be immensely richer for the contact. Fox believes the gamble is worth it. He believes we will meet aliens, sometime, and that they will be good. But Fox is one man against millions. He talks, but nobody listens, but he goes on hoping that he'll be the one to make contact. Call him a fanatic, if you want to. I happen to think he's right."

Lambert stood up slowly. "That's why I don't like what I'm hearing around the ship. The men are getting panicky in spite of all the psych conditioning they've had, and in spite of all the care that went into selecting the crew for this mission. They're the best possible men in their jobs, and still they're panicky. To me, that means only one thing."

Lars felt the knot in his stomach again. "What?"

"Somebody on board is deliberately setting off the panic. Somebody who's smart enough to keep under cover himself and put the words into other peoples' mouths. I think you know who, too."

Lars was silent for a long time. Then he said, "I guess I do. But why? Why should he want to do it?"

"You find out that answer in time and you might save this ship a whole lot of trouble," Lambert said heavily. "Because we're heading for trouble now faster than we're heading for Wolf IV."

The talking was worse than Lars realized. The tension in the ship had grown tremendously since he had dug into the work in the lab. In small groups lurking in the corridors, in hasty words passed across the eating bar in the galley, in looks, nods, and whispers trouble was spelled out in large letters.

There was Jeff Salter, talking to the assistant engineer and the radioman down in the lounge, with a wary eye out for intruders, saying, "We've been shanghaied, that's what happened. You know what that means." And, "Old Foxy hasn't any legal right to force us into it. We signed contracts, you know." And, "Guinea pigs! That's what he's making us. You guys eager to be heroes? I'm not."

And in the corridor outside sleeping quarters, muffled voices, saying, "Fox doesn't care what happens to the ship *or* the men. It's the glory for himself he wants."

Or, "—couldn't get a crew to sign up the regular way, that's what it means."

Or, "Sure he's Commander, but he's beyond his rights, I tell you! No court on Earth would back him up if the facts were known."

And behind it all, always present here or there, was Peter Brigham, never saying much, only a word here, a malicious grin there, a question at the right moment in another place.

And Tom Lorry, worry heavy on his quizzical face as he went about the ship, showing the strain and trying to hide it, trying to grasp the full meaning of the tension that built up, and not quite succeeding.

And Paul Morehouse, navigator, his usually affable expression gone, lines of worry on his face too as he checked the bearings and recalculated the course, underscored the day's progress for his report to the skipper.

And Walter Fox, his pale blue eyes alert, but always firm, always confident as he moved about the ship, checking preparations, a nod here, a smile there, oblivious to the cold looks, the short answers, the whispers.

Another day, more whispers, new complaints. Peter Brigham carefully avoiding Lars now, rising before Lars awoke, never in the bunkroom, always in a group in the lounge, never alone.

Lars found him at last, just turning in as another sleep period began. He snapped the light off quickly as Lars pushed open the hatch, but Lars snapped it on again, and walked slowly to his locker. He started to undress.

"What do you think you're doing?" he asked suddenly, turning on Peter. "Come on, you're not asleep. Answer me! What do you think you're doing?"

Peter looked up at him lazily. "Old Eagle-eye! Been watching me, have you?"

"You bet I have."

"All right, then you tell me. What am I doing?"

"Look, this is no joke," Lars said. "You've got the men on this ship ready to fly apart any minute. Don't you know what's happening? Can't you see what comes next?"

Peter sat up suddenly, and he wasn't smiling. His eyes were intent on Lars' face. "No, tell me what comes next."

"Mutiny comes next. And you know it as well as I do. You've been doing everything in your power to turn this crew against Commander Fox. You've put the words in their mouths, the ideas in their heads. And if you play your cards just right, you're going to succeed, too."

Peter roared with laughter, his arms gripping his sides as he rolled on the bunk. "And you're just getting the idea *now?* Where have you been?" He caught his breath, his laughter dying as suddenly as it started. "But that's all right, that's all right. It it's soaked through to your level, it *must* be working!"

"Working!"

"Yes, working. I told you Fox had some questions to answer, didn't I? Well, I meant it. He hasn't even started answering yet."

"But *mutiny*—"

"It'll make this one thing certain," said Peter Brigham through his teeth, "that Walter Fox will never lift another Star Ship off Earth, *ever*. Even if it takes a mutiny to stop him."

5

NO PLACE FOR COWARDS

FOR A long moment there was silence as Lars stared at Peter. Then, slowly, he sank down on the bench along the bulkhead. "So it's *Fox* you're after," he said. "Not the place the ship is going, or what we may find there. You're not concerned about that at all, just about getting Walter Fox."

"Now you're getting the idea," said Peter.

Lars shook his head. "I don't get it. Peter, it just doesn't make *sense*, what you're doing. You're taking the greatest planet-breaker that Earth ever sent to space, and you're trying to mutiny his crew and break him. Why? Whom could we have in command better than Fox? He's led crews into unknown territory before, and they've trusted him, and he's brought them back, too. Don't you *know* what Fox has done?"

"Oh, yes, I know all right. You're the one who doesn't." Peter gave Lars a scornful glance. "You're so sick with hero-worship you wouldn't recognize the truth about Walter Fox if it walked up and kicked you in the teeth. I don't know why I even bother talking to you."

"I know that Fox is a great man, if that's what you mean, and I'm proud to be aboard his ship."

"I know, I know," Peter sighed. "You've read his books, and all the nice newspaper reports of his voyages, all singularly favorable to Walter Fox. Big press releases, fancy live 3-V broadcasts, everything. That's your idea of the man."

"And your idea?"

"That he's a fanatic and a fool," Peter snapped. "Why do you think this ship was ever commissioned on this trip in the first place? Because Fox knew about the *Planetfall* and screamed to high heaven until they gave him a ship and men to go hunt her down. Why was he so eager? Because of the *Planetfall*, do you think? Fox didn't care two beans about the *Planetfall*. But he smelled aliens, and that meant he had to come, no matter how he managed it or whom he brought along. Handing him a ship and sending him to Wolf IV was like handing a knife to a homicidal maniac and turning him loose on the town."

"I don't believe it," Lars said slowly.

"How could you? You've only looked at one side of the nickel. The news broadcasts don't tell you the other side: that Fox is so obsessed with this idea of first contact with aliens that he runs his crews into the ground in order to satisfy it. He's lost more crewmen than any other major explorer, and do you know why? Because he isn't satisfied with finding good colony sites and then bringing his ship home again to let the ground-breakers take over. He's got to scour every planet for evidence of intelligent life. If he kills half his crew doing it, that's just too bad."

Lars stared, horrified at the virulence in Peter's voice. "You really hate him, don't you?"

Peter's mouth twisted. "I hate everything he stands for."

"But it's more than that," said Lars. "It's wrong, it doesn't fit you, somehow. I can remember you back in school, always putting on this show of sarcasm, acting as if you hated everybody and everything, and yet you nearly flunked your finals last year because you spent all cram-week coaching little Barnes, who was on probation and flunking out."

Peter shrugged impatiently. "He'd have flunked for sure if he hadn't had help."

"Yes, but you gave him help. All that sarcasm and bitterness was just a phoney act when the chips were down with Barnes, weren't they, Peter?"

"All right, so I'm no angel in disguise."

"Not by a long way, but now you're putting this whole crew in jeopardy just to cut Walter Fox's throat for him. It doesn't add up, Peter. I'm slow, but I'm not blind. And all these stories about Fox and his crews on exploratories."

Peter was on his feet, his eyes blazing. "They're true!" he cried. "They're true. You just don't know. You think he's great, but he's cruel and stupid and *bad*." Suddenly his voice was different; the sarcasm and arrogance were gone, and he was sincere, almost pleading. "Look. Just listen to me for a minute. There was a landing on Arcturus IV ten years ago, maybe eleven, do you remember? That was the first time a ship had landed there, the prelims had warned against it, but Fox went down. He could have flown the surface in an observation craft, but he was afraid they might miss something on the surface. He thought he had found evidence of an alien on that planet, so he led his crew through a hundred miles of dust storm and desert without proper protection from the sun, without adequate food or water.

"Fox didn't find his alien, but when the crew got back to the ship all of them had radiation burns, and three of them were dead. No, you didn't read the whole story of that trip, because they never published it. They were afraid they'd scare away colonists. They got their colony going, too, but the three men who died didn't come back to life. They put up a monument to them on Arcturus IV, and then forgot them and the trip just as fast as they could."

"Wait a minute," Lars said. "I read the log of that trip. There was something about dust-devils—"

"You mean Fox's obsession. Maybe you remember the names of the men that died."

"One was Markovsky, he was the engineer. And there was Lindell and—"

Lars' jaw dropped, and he stared at Peter.

"Go on," said Peter.

"I—didn't know—"

"Three names on a gravestone," said Peter. "Markovsky and Lindell and Brigham. Thomas Brigham, navigator on the *Star Ship Mimas* under Walter Fox. My father."

Somewhere in the corridor beyond a time-bell chimed. Far below them the engines of the ship shifted subtly, driving the vibrating thrum-thrum-thrum a fraction faster. Occasionally they heard a voice above them, the clang of a boot on metal plates, familiar sounds of a ship en route, for a Star Ship is never silent. But in the tiny bunkroom it seemed for a moment that a separate world existed.

"I didn't know," said Lars.

"Of course you didn't." Peter's voice was surprisingly gentle, a gentleness Lars had never heard from him. It struck him even harder than the words Peter had blurted out a moment before. He had known Peter only by the shell, the anger and bitterness and arrogance. But now, suddenly, he knew that all this had only been a shell, and slowly Lars began to understand things. Things that he had wondered about many times before, things he had never understood about the slender, dark-haired youth he had disliked so much.

Before, he had only seen the hatred that Peter had shown to the world; now, with sudden understanding, he saw the misery and loneliness that lay behind the hatred. He had a mental picture of a boy, maybe ten years old, receiving the news that his father was dead somewhere, on some far planet. The news created a void that nothing ever again could fill. Then he saw the boy, older, questioning, wondering, having to know why his father had died, impatient in his loss and misery with the published reports, seeking out other crewmen, questioning—

True answers? Or false? It didn't matter. All that mattered was the need to strike back, to hate the world that had killed his father, to hate the man who had been responsible. But hatred is a vicious thing, spreading and tainting everything it touches, twisting and hiding the good that it obscures.

Lars saw it clearly, and shook his head in wonder. "You were determined to get aboard the *Ganymede,* then. To get to Fox some way, any way."

"I had to get aboard," Peter said. "If I hadn't made it this time, I would have the next, or the next. There are lots of men named Brigham. Fox would never know until I got ready to tell him. I had to do it. He's got to be stopped, somehow, and I'm going to stop him."

"But what about the rest?"

Peter's lips tightened. "I've got to stop Fox. I'm sorry about the rest, but I can't help it."

"It's wrong, Peter."

"He'll never take another Star Ship off Earth."

"But can't you see that you're taking it out on every man aboard?"

"I don't see how. We'll turn him back. They won't have to go to Wolf IV, unless they want to, the next trip, with a man who's fit to lead them."

"Suppose you're right about Fox, and suppose you *don't* turn him back? Then what? Landing on Wolf IV with half the crew in irons, with no morale at all, with everybody afraid of everybody else—" Lars shook his head. "You could destroy every man on the ship, if you keep this up. Even a mutiny in itself, why, the men are sitting on knife-edges up there! Suppose they jumped the gun, tried to take the ship without enough support, at the wrong time. There'd be fighting, Peter. How many are going to be killed, because you want to get Walter Fox? And those that got back, do you think Earth courts would back up a mutiny? The ones that got back would be in for lifetime demolition."

Peter's face was pale. He looked at Lars for a long moment. Then "I'm sorry. If there was a better way—"

"But there *is!*"

"What?"

"Look, I don't know if you're right or wrong about Commander Fox. I just don't know. But I do know that he's stepped over the line legally on this trip. Anything we do now is criminal, because he's the law on his Star Ship in space. All right. We back him up now. We go to Wolf IV and find the *Planetfall* if she's there to be found. Then when we get home we press every charge against him that we can dream up, and press it to the hilt. Kidnapping, conspiracy, incompetence—anything with any grounds at all. *When we get home,* Peter, with a crack space lawyer and all the trimmings."

"I can't back him now. Not on anything. I just can't."

"All right, then don't, but don't fight him. If you fight him, *nobody* may get home. You'll have to move fast. Salter is getting the whole ship aroused, and you'll have to stop him somehow, but it's the only thing to do. We can get Fox when it's all over."

Peter looked at Lars. "We?"

"If you'll stop this panic you've started and go along, I'll back you to the hilt when we get home."

"You give me your word?"

"You've got it."

Peter scratched his jaw. "I might be able to slow it up. Salter is the one who's talking the loudest, but they're ready to blow any time. I'll have to move fast."

The lights in the bunkroom went out.

Somewhere above them were sounds of shouts and running feet, and a hatchway clanged shut. Peter jumped up from his bunk, listening. They heard more shouts and a shot.

"Too late!" he whispered.

The wall-speaker crackled, and Tom Lorry's voice roared out:

"All hands, man your stations. Every man get to his station at once. This ship is now on emergency military orders—"

The voice was choked off and the speaker went dead.

"The hold!" Peter cried. "They'll try to get to the engines—" And then he and Lars were running pell-mell down the dark corridor, wrist-lights flashing, and the thought ran again and again through Lars' mind: *It's too late! It's already too late!*

* * *

What happened then came so fast that Lars never was sure of the sequence. There were a series of impressions—bodies moving, lights flashing, men shouting, the clanging of the battle stations bell. He was rushing through darkness, following Peter Brigham's bouncing wrist-light down a hatch, along a corridor and down into another hatch, black as pitch. Suddenly his light showed no floor, no wall, only a thin metal railing and a catwalk. Lars gasped, dizzy, as his boots went ping-ping-ping on the metal lathing. Then Peter disappeared before him, and Lars groped at the end of the catwalk for metal ladder rungs.

A metal floor-plate, a walkway leading toward the hulking black engines, their hum a frantic scream in his ears now. Peter stopped, panting, peering into the darkness, and their ears caught more footsteps on the catwalk above, a curse, a flicker of light.

"Back here!" Peter whispered, and jerked Lars along the walkway. It formed a bridge between the engine controls and the catwalk ladder. Three men, maybe more, were coming down the ladder now, starting up the walkway.

"Hold it!" Peter's voice cut out in the darkness. His light flickered on their faces. Jeff Salter was in the lead. Behind him was Bob Tenebreck, the geologist, and another man.

Salter stopped short, poised. "Brigham? Get out of the way. We've got to get those engines."

"It's no good, Jeff. Fox was onto it. He was ready. We can't pull it off."

"I can damn well pull those engines off!" Salter roared. "That'll throw everybody off their feet for a while."

"It's not the right time!" Peter's voice was urgent. "You've got to call it off."

Jeff Salter's thin face twisted. "Get out of my way. I'm coming through there."

He moved straight for them, the other following. Lars pushed Peter aside like a feather and met Salter with a full body block. His broad shoulder crashed into the thin man's chest, hurling him backward. Salter leaped to his feet with a roar and charged. Lars met him hard with a right that spun his head around, and followed with a left to the body. Salter crumpled to the floor, groaning. But Tenebreck caught Lars hard in the shoulder, spinning him into the other man's fist. The fist connected before Lars could wriggle loose and strike out at both assailants. Tenebreck fell to his knees, scrambled back up with a snarl and met Lars' fist full in the mouth. He dropped so hard his head clanged on the floor plate.

The third man glared at Lars, hesitating to close on him. "Come on," Lars growled through his teeth. "You waiting for help?"

Suddenly the lights flashed on, and Lorry's voice bellowed from the catwalk:

"All right, you! Stand where you are!"

Lorry scrambled down the ladder, a machine pistol tight in his fist. Paul Morehouse followed him, eyeing the two men on the floor in surprise. Lorry moved quickly, patting Peter's pockets. Then he nodded to Morehouse. "Clean. You stop them?" This was to Lars.

Lars swallowed and nodded.

"He helping you?" He jerked a thumb at Peter.

Lars nodded again.

"Uh. Well, you'd better wipe off your chin. You look like you were chewing them to death. Now get up to the lounge, and lug these creeps along with you." He glared at Salter and Tenebreck, who were climbing to their feet. "Nothing funny now, or you'll regret it."

Salter groaned, clutching his head. Lorry grinned at Lars. "Come on, Horatio. Give him a hand."

The gathering in the lounge was tense and angry. Commander Fox was there, his face white, his lips cutting a thin line across his face. Lorry, Morehouse, Lambert and Kennedy, the photographer, were armed with machine pistols; Kennedy's arm was in an improvised sling, the white cloth stained with blood.

Across the room, sullen and pale, stood Salter and Tenebreck and half a dozen others. There was no talking. They glared at Fox, but had nothing to say. The mutiny attempt, such as it was, had failed.

"All right, how many of you were in on this mess?" Fox asked, looking from man to man.

Nobody answered. Several of the men looked at their feet. Fox grimaced. "So. You've done a great job, the lot of you. You didn't quite get the ship from me, but you split it as wide open as you could." His eyes stopped on Peter. "A fine job."

There was silence. Feet shuffled. Fox walked back and forth like a tiger in a cage. "All right, if you don't want to talk, I'll talk. I run a peaceful ship. I give the orders on it, and my men obey those orders and back me up on the jobs I have to do. If they don't want it that way, they get off my ship. All right. Now some of you boys don't seem to like things the way they are. Salter? You've been doing a lot of talking. Let's hear what you have to say, right out in the open so everybody can hear it. Come on, sound off!"

"We've been sold a bill of goods, and we don't like it," Salter growled. "You've got no legal right to hold us here against our will, and you know it. We don't want to be guinea pigs in this alien hunt of yours. We don't want any part of it."

"Who's this 'we' you're talking about?"

"The majority of the crew," Salter snapped. "They all think the same, and they don't want any more of your pep talks, either."

"Then just what *do* you want?"

"We want to turn back."

"So that's the way it is, eh?" Fox looked around the group. "Leeds? Do you go along with that?"

"I go along with Salter," the big engineer said. "I didn't bargain for this kind of trip when I signed aboard."

"Carpenter?"

"I say turn back."

"Mangano?"

"Turn back."

"All right, let's get the whole crew in on this. How many of you go with Salter?"

There was an angry rumble, and hands went into the air. Lars clenched his fists at his sides, counted seven hands, then saw an eighth hesitantly go up. Peter's hand was down.

"And with me?"

Again hands went up: Lorry's, Morehouse's, Lambert's, half a dozen others. Lars raised his hand in the air.

"Brigham? How about you?"

"I'm not voting," Peter said quietly.

"This is the wrong time to ride the fence."

"I'm not voting."

"Mr. Lorry, what's the count."

"Eight with Salter, thirteen with you, one abstains."

Fox turned his eyes to Peter for a long moment; then with a growl of disgust he turned to Salter. "Seems like you've been listening to the wrong advice," he said slowly. "Well now you're going to face a few facts. This trip to

Wolf IV wasn't my idea. I didn't volunteer the ship, or the men. Colonial Service picked me, and outfitted me, because there was a job that had to be done. It may be a very dirty job, but it *has to be done*."

He leaned back against the table, his face grim. "The Colonial Service has its back to the wall. An alien scare back home would be a disaster. It would mean an end to the colonization program that Earth has to have. The Service knew that the *Planetfall* has to be found, and we've got the job of finding her. It doesn't matter whether we like the job or not, we've got to do it with all the resources at our command. That means we can't carry dead wood. There's no place for cowards on this ship now. Am I making myself clear?"

Jeff Salter's face was pale. "You can't throw us off the ship in deep space!"

"I can, and I will."

"That's murder."

"You can call it anything you like," Fox said harshly. "Nevertheless, you have a choice, you eight. You've attempted a mutiny on this ship. Okay. I'm willing to overlook it because I need men and I need skills on Wolf IV. You can go along with me in landing there and back me up one hundred per cent in the search for the *Planetfall*, or you can have one lifeboat for the eight of you and two weeks' food and water, and we'll break the Koenig field long enough to jettison you. That's your choice. Think it over. You've got ten seconds."

The men stared at him, and at Salter. Even Lars could hardly believe the harshness of the Commander's decree.

It was no choice. It was a death sentence.

"All right," Salter said dully. "We'll back you."

"I don't mean any half-hearted motions. I mean full

support. If there's any break at all, the eight of you pay for it."

"We'll back you."

"All right. Get back to your stations. Mr. Morehouse says we'll make the Wolf system in record time. There's plenty of work to be done in the meantime. And if we're lucky, some of us may even leave the place alive."

6

THE GRAY PLANET

TIME IS amazingly compressible.

Like the hypothetical "perfect gas," a day can be pressed down into a second, or expanded to last a lifetime. It seemed to Lars Heldrigsson that the few short days since the *Ganymede* blasted from Earth had lasted for eons; now, even with the artificially designated day periods and sleep periods, the days and weeks sped by with unimaginable speed.

There was work—long hours of study, equipment testing, procedure-rehearsal, conference, preparation and planning. Every man on the ship filled a hole in the fabric; every man had to be prepared for anything that might impinge on his specialized field of knowledge. There would be no time for preparation when the time for landfall arrived. The success of the mission, their very lives, depended upon what they did *now,* before destination, before the unknown was faced.

The old tradition that the weeks en route on a Star Ship were a leisurely time for the crewmen to while away, get on each other's nerves and scrap with each other was a snare and a delusion of staggering proportions. Lars would have laughed at the thought, if he had had time to think about it, but he didn't.

Not that everything was sweetness and harmony. There was still talking and complaining. No one could really forget that a mutiny had been attempted, nor could they forget the choice that the Commander had laid down for the insurgents. There were bitter feelings, angry words, but even these faded away in the weight of the work that had to be done. There wasn't time to be bitter, or angry. There wasn't time to talk. There was a job that took the skill and wit of every man on the crew, and the job had to be done first.

Their lives hung on it. They knew that, to a man.

Kennedy, the photographer and mapper, buried himself in the photolab, rolling the film strips, checking the camera synchronizations, checking again and again the special film-sensitivities, preparing the tiny photo-scooter with its four giant multi-lensed 3-V cameras for the initial runs on the planet. Dorffman, the radioman, worked with him in the craft, setting up the delicate beaming mechanisms that Kennedy would depend upon for contact with the ship, then retiring to his own shop to prepare the sampler-units that would be sent down for the first remote contact with the surface of Wolf IV. In the maze of catwalks and bridges in the engine rooms Mangano and Leeds labored to get the auxiliary engines, the auxiliary power supplies, the portable powerpacks and generators into condition for use in all emergency circumstances. Paul Morehouse spent hours with Salter and Peter Brigham, working out landing procedures, setting up special problems to be solved, checking timing and coordination and accuracy, until he was satisfied that either of them could handle the ship with skill in any emergency that might arise.

The ship was emergency tuned. She was tense and poised with the dampered eagerness of a greyhound at the bar. Her crew had one goal to reach, one charge to fulfill to the limit of human ability: *be ready for anything*.

They had to be, and they knew it. As the weeks passed and the ship sped on, there was no way to escape the knowledge.

No one dug in harder than Peter Brigham. Where he had turned his cleverness to troublemaking before, now he was the pacifier, and if there was an edge to his peacemaking nobody noticed it in particular. In fact, to Lars the change was remarkable. Peter maintained his sarcastic tongue and his arrogant manner to the rest of the crew, but to Lars he was different. They talked now where they had bickered. There was no further reference to Lars' slowness; one rest period Peter listened with something approaching admiration as Lars told him the problems that were faced and overcome daily by a Greenland wheat farmer if he wanted to stay alive.

And Lars in turn was amazed at the store of information in his new friend's head. To Lars curiosity had always been a luxury; he had been too busy mastering his own narrow field to wander far astray. But Peter's curiosity was all-consuming. He had read far more than Lars had imagined, and more remarkable yet, he had, occasionally, thought about what he had read.

"Now you take the teleps, for instance," Peter said one

sleep period as they lay in the bunkroom. "The youngsters they have on 3-V, tossing the teledice around like they were alive, and reading card-packs like magicians. A lot of people think they're freaks, some sort of weird misfits that just don't behave like normal people."

"Well, aren't they? You don't see me going around trying to read minds, do you?" Lars yawned.

"No, and yet everybody knows that mothers and their babies read each other's minds like books. Well, all right, not very well, maybe, but there's *something* in contact there. I sometimes wonder if everybody isn't a little bit telep."

Lars chuckled. "If you could read my mind right now, you'd get pretty sore."

"Well, they *used* to think that. Back in the Great War Age, men like Rhine were even trying to prove it scientifically. Of course, they got laughed out of existence, but you can't help wondering."

"You go ahead and wonder. I'm going to sleep." Lars turned to the wall, still chuckling.

"I used to know what my father was thinking," Peter said doggedly. "I swear I did."

And once again Lars was jerked back to the story Peter had told him of the expedition to Arcturus IV. Peter had worshiped his father; it was no wonder that he had built up a burning hatred for the man he believed was responsible for his death. And yet now he worked his full share on Walter Fox's ship and never mentioned Fox. "Go to sleep," Lars said gently. "There's work to be done tomorrow."

He was indeed a prophet, if without honor. Four hours later the Koenig drive lapsed and threw the *Ganymede* into control of the atomic-thrust engines.

The ship had entered the system of the star called Wolf.

* * *

They hit a stable orbit 500 miles out from the planet and started Schedule I rolling like a well-oiled precision robot. Ever present in the black space-void, the huge orange sun that was the star Wolf glared balefully at them, like an angry giant, half-slumbering, half-aware that intruders were near. Below them was the fourth planet, a dim gray sphere that lay featureless and silent in its cradle of blackness, reflecting the light of its sun in orange-grayness sometimes, blotting out the stars in blackness at other times. When the planet eclipsed the sun the lead-gray color became pit-black. Only occasionally was there a break in its gray blanket, allowing a glimpse of surface beneath.

Kennedy's cameras ground continuously, the little man's face buried for hours at a time in the view box of the telescopic scanner as Commander Fox took a place beside him, trying to penetrate, to find any detail, any suggestion of the nature of the planet.

"Clouds," Kennedy growled again and again. "Nothing. Even haze filters won't break them."

"Something coming now," Fox said. "Watch it."

"Yeah. Polar cap. And now there's a break down below —brother! Ice halfway down to the equator. She's a cold baby, that planet. Got the heat suits in shape?"

Fox grinned humorlessly. "Dorffman? Any signs of life?"

The radioman shook his head. "Nothing."

"Don't drop it. How about the radar?"

"No signal of anything. Not even meteors to shake us up some."

"Keep in touch with that screen. If anything shoots up, I want to know it yesterday."

"Right. Want me to bounce a couple down there?"

Fox scratched his jaw. "A thought, at that. I don't think so. The more we know before we're spotted the better."

"Might tell us what we want to know."

"Might blow us out of the sky, too. Patience, lad." He flipped a switch. "Lambert?"

"Nothing for you, Commander."

Kennedy pushed back from the viewer. "Gotta get closer."

"Nothing at all on the films?"

"Afraid not."

"All right. Paul, drop us in closer."

They broke orbit, and the lead-gray sphere began to swell, to flatten as they moved. Still there was no sign. No aircraft rose from the surface; no signals went up. The planet might have been dead, but the cloud blankets were thicker than ever, hiding, obscuring.

They took a new orbit at 150 miles. "All right," said Fox. "Get the scouts out and let's get busy."

They got busy.

Lambert brought in a prelim on the other planets while Lars still checked and rechecked details. "This may help some. No. I planet is in close and hot, comparable to our Mercury. II and III are twins and carry no atmosphere to speak of. V and VI are far out and cold, ammonia-methane atmosphere. Looks like IV is the only planet of Wolf with anything like a plausible atmosphere, at least as far as humans are concerned."

"No possibility that Millar took his ship down on one of the others?"

"Not a shade."

"Then let's poke a finger down there. Got your scout ready?"

The snub-nosed servo broke free of the ship and slid down in a descending orbit, moving in slow downward spirals and vanishing into the cloud blanket. Dorffman sat alert at the radio controls and hissed through his teeth. "Something wrong, I think."

"What is it?"

"Magnetic storm. It's fierce! I'm losing it. No, there it is. But it's not stable. Either these instruments are way off or that atmosphere is wild."

The men crowded around him as he moved the controls. Far below the servo scooped up surface air and surface dirt, measured tremperature, pressure, gravitation, wind velocity. Dorffman started it up again, and swore. They spotted it instants later, a bright metal chip zooming upward in a wildly erratic course, finally stabilizing and homing on the receiver slot in the *Ganymede*. Robot fingers opened it, transferred air and soil samples to flasks and culture plates. Then Lars and Lambert got busy.

Kennedy groaned as cloud banks whirled by below him.

"Only a little peek once in a while. I'd better take the scooter down."

"All right. Go to it. But fifty miles is the limit, and get back here fast if there's a peep of trouble. Keep whispering in Dorffman's ear."

They watched him slide down in the camera-scooter, heard his signals to Dorffman dissolve into a rattle of indistinguishable static as he hit the atmosphere. They sweated him out six hours until he homed in, weary and disgusted.

"No good?" asked Fox.

He shook his head. "Nothing of value. We were right about the ice cap. Squares with the temp readings, too, mean equatorial temperature is about 4° Centigrade. There are oceans at the equator, and a long continental land mass. Maybe the next run will give me more."

The next run didn't and neither did the next or the next. But Kennedy kept trying.

Lars reported the atmosphere analysis. "Oxygen 16.8, carbon dioxide 0.8, nitrogen 81.3. Inert gases make up the rest. No trace of sulphur or chlorine or organic gases. It's a breathable atmosphere even if it's a little short of O_2."

"Radioactivity?"

"Some latent activity, but it's negligible. No concentration we can spot."

"How about micro-organisms?"

"They're there, but they grow cold; 5° is their optimum. They won't live in our mice, and Lambert doubts that there's any possibility of contamination, but we're making vaccines just the same. No sense in being heroes."

Fox gave him a tired smile and went back to the close films from Kennedy's last run. He had slept little if any in the week they had been orbited, and he felt weariness in every muscle. Frame after frame flickered before his eyes, sterile, empty of information.

"All right," he said finally. "Get the boys together. From here on in we're up to our necks." He gave Kennedy a hopeless look. "No sign of the *Planetfall* in any of the films?"

"Not a sign." There was no hesitation in Kennedy's voice.

"That's what I like about you," Fox said. "You're so honest."

Council of War.

Every man was present, and every man was tense. In the welter of detail work it had been easy to forget the broader picture, to thrust out of their minds where they were, why they were there, what they had to do there. But that was over now.

"We've gotten everything we can get up here, and we have nothing. Some physical data, incomplete; some looks at the surface, so sketchy they're useless. We have no data that helps us."

"No positive data," Kennedy corrected him. "We've got plenty of negative data."

"You mean the fact that nothing has tried to shoot us out of the sky?" Fox shrugged. "That's not much comfort, I'm afraid."

"More than that. No evidence at all that Wolf IV is any kind of going concern. Not a peep, not a picture. And also, we know the *Planetfall* couldn't have landed anywhere else. Not in this system."

Fox looked around at the men. "Still not much to go on. Schedule I is a blank for all practical purposes. So we move into Schedule II. We've got to put the ship down there."

There was a stir about the room.

Lambert took his pipe out of his mouth. "Bio division can't find any reason not to set down. We know there's microscopic flora, safe, and surface vegetation. Also insect life, pretty low order. I can't militate against a landing. Still—"

"Well?" Fox looked at him sharply.

"We still don't know what we're going to do when we get down there. We know we land on the equator, period. We might as well walk in blindfolded."

"Granted," said Fox.

"If there are aliens down there, they may be set to mop us up in twenty minutes flat. They may just be waiting."

"Well, what do you suggest?"

Suddenly Peter Brigham spoke up. "Seems to me we're ignoring one very important fact."

"What's that?"

"That nothing happened to the *Planetfall* until she was on the ground with the crew dispersed. She went through her routine Schedule I just the way we have, and apparently didn't see anything to scare her off. Looks to me as though we could orbit out here for fifty years and get no farther than we are now."

There were nods of agreement, reluctant nods. Lambert lit his pipe again. Jeff Salter scraped his jaw with his hand and looked unhappy.

"There's one thing we can still do," Kennedy said at last. "We need a close look down there, a *good* look. Let me take the scooter down close, three or four thousand feet, and see if I can't get some decent films. Then at least we could land on solid ground."

Fox nodded. "You want to try it?"

"You bet I do."

"Then get moving. The rest of you hit the sack for a while. I want some of you half-awake when Kennedy gets back. We may not get any sleep for a while after we've landed."

No one disputed the wisdom of Fox's words, but no one slept. They watched the little photographer slide the scooter out of her slot and zoom down toward the gray planet to vanish into the cloud bank. Dorffman stayed rooted to the beam receiver, struggling to keep contact, but the signals got weaker and more garbled by the second and finally disintegrated into occasional bursts of nonsense-squawking. Dorffman shook his head, and tried to sleep in his headset.

They waited. A card game started up, but didn't get very far. Lars puttered in the lab, trying to pretend interest, and finally went back to the observation booth to join the others. An hour passed, and another.

"How long was he supposed to take?" Mangano asked peevishly.

"Fox said a four-hour limit. If he isn't back by then, we go down after him."

"Silly fool asked for it," Salter grumbled.

"It had to be done," Lars snapped.

"Yeah, sure."

Three hours passed; three and a half, with no sign of the camera-scooter. Dorffman was getting no signals at all now. He swore and cut in on a different band, sweat standing in beads on his forehead.

On the wall the speaker crackled. "Lorry, Morehouse, Lambert, better come aft to the lifeboats. He's got twenty minutes more. If he's not back, we'll take two boats down."

Below them a vile gray dawn was moving across the planet's face. The star Wolf glowered an evil orange. The men were silent now, staring through the viewports, hardly breathing.

There was a glint of light below, the whine of a jet engine, and a sudden crackle of static from the receiver, mellowing out into a readable signal. The men let out a cheer as the scooter rose from the clouds and began homing on the Star Ship. Minutes later it clanged into its slot, and Kennedy crawled from the cockpit, weary and pale but very much alive. He threw off his heater-suit with a groan, but his eyes were bright with excitement.

"The films!" Fox exploded. "Did you get films? Could you see anything?"

"Find a poor man a beer, if you can," groaned Kennedy. "Better yet, coffee. I want to sit down." He grinned at the men around him, and then said, "I got films, all right. Miles of films. I followed a break in the weather clear around that dirty ball, and I filmed her, by Jupiter. But you'll want to see my last reel first."

"You saw something?"

"I saw enough to shut me up for the rest of my life," said Kennedy. "I saw more than enough. Including the wreck of the *Planetfall*." He hesitated, an odd look on his face. "But it was something else I saw that threw me. I just hope my camera saw it too."

7

PETER MAKES A CHOICE

THE WHOLE crew was crowding around Bob Kennedy now as he drank coffee and got himself warm. Here at last was something tangible, something the men could grasp, some clear-cut and indisputable fact in the midst of a sea of uncertainty. But Kennedy would say nothing more until the film reels were unloaded from the cameras and fed into the processing baths. "Those are my eyes," he insisted doggedly. "They'll tell you better than I can exactly what I saw down there."

"But you saw the *Planetfall,*" the Commander said.

"I saw the *wreck* of the *Planetfall*. At least it looked like a wreck from the glimpse or two I got of it. And you'll never bring the *Ganymede* down close to her. She's spread all over the mountainside in what looked like almost inaccessible country. In fact—" the photographer blinked owlishly at the navigator, "—Paul is going to have a time landing this crate anywhere on that planet. There's only one continental land mass, lying on the equator, and almost every bit of it looks vicious. Mountains and storms. Gorges cutting a mile deep. Only one river, and that looks bigger than our Amazon. It drains the whole mountain range. And the whole country is covered with the meanest looking jungle I ever set eyes on."

"Jungle? In that climate?" It was Lambert's turn to look surprised.

"Wait until you see the pictures."

Lambert lit his pipe thoughtfully. "If there's a river of that size, there's a delta."

"That's right, and that looked like the only reasonable landing place," Kennedy affirmed. "But I wouldn't like to navigate this boat down on it, and it'll put us a good seventy-five miles from the wreck in the mountains."

"Did you see anything suggesting survivors?" Fox asked.

Kennedy hesitated. "Let's look at the films, shall we? The wreck I saw looked cold as a wedge, but there was a valley over a pass from where it lay, and what I saw there—well, I'm not just so sure *what* I saw."

"What do you mean by that?"

"It looked like a city," said Kennedy slowly.

Commander Fox stared at him. "A *city!* Are you certain?"

"No, I'm not. Not by a long sight. Look, let me just run through it briefly." The photographer refilled his coffee cup and rubbed his forehead wearily. "I broke through the clouds just over this river, and I spent some time following it up into the rough mountain country. We'll have to trek up into that place, Commander. I wouldn't take the risk of setting even my scooter down there. The weather was terrible, but I got some good shots of the terrain, and I think you'll agree. Anyway, I lost the river when it broke into smaller streams, and was just debating whether I should try to find a pass over the mountains from that level or go up higher when I saw something up on the ridge. I kept it low, and nearly killed myself ramming the ridge because of the fog, but I finally got a close look. There was *something* that didn't belong there, and on my final pass I got a clear look at the jets and fins of a Star Ship sticking up out of a snowbank high on the ridge. Then I saw chunks of hull-plate and smashed-up engines spread for five miles in all directions. And as far as I'm concerned, that's the end of the *Planetfall*. Nobody could have survived a crash like that."

There was tense silence. Then Fox said, "But the city—"

"I was coming to that. I had to scout for another hour to find a pass over the ridge, but I found one, and got through under the weather to a high plateau-like valley on the other side. I was just going to take a quick run, and then come back here when I saw it down there, and I thought my eyes were going bad on me. I thought I saw buildings through a break in the clouds. I had the cameras going full tilt, and made another pass, and then half a dozen more, and every time I saw something, all right, but it never looked the same twice. It seemed to be shifting all over the place, and then I couldn't find it at all."

Commander Fox scowled. "Now look, a city doesn't go bouncing all over the countryside."

"Maybe not, but that's exactly what this thing was doing."

"Let's look at the films."

The first ones were dry enough for viewing. Lars helped Paul Morehouse set up the projector, and soon they were watching the jerking landscape flowing by on the 3-V screen as Kennedy stood by to identify the locations.

It chilled every man to watch those films. Lars caught himself shivering and wishing they were watching the old flatties that never put the viewer quite so much in the picture. It looked *cold* out there, cold with a savage bitterness that the bleakest winters on Earth could not match. The land was gray and cruel-looking, with jagged mountain crests and long rugged stretches of wind-bitten gray-green vegetation spread out like a jungle, clinging fungus-like to the rocky land. They saw the river, yellow-gray, torrential as it raced down the mountainsides, spreading out onto a broad delta where it met the gray sea. There seemed to be trails through the jungle, but there were only momentary glimpses of these. Certainly there was nothing resembling a road.

Then the camera's eye turned up into the mountains, and they caught a silvery flash in the distance. Kennedy ran through long strips of film eagerly. "Here, now," he said. "I got it better a little farther along—there!"

Lars stopped the projector, and they gazed at the fuzzy picture. It stood out clearly from its surroundings, the wrecked hull of a Star Ship, its nose buried deep in snow and rubble on the high, rocky ridge, the great yawning holes of its jets rising up like another crag to meet the wind. Snow drifted into the gaping airlock. There was no sign of life anywhere about it.

"The *Planetfall,*" Jeff Salter said heavily. "Commander, what more do you want to know? This is what we came here to find. We've found her. They were wrecked in landing. Nobody could have survived. Any fool can see that this planet is hopeless as a colony site. Why risk waiting any longer?"

"What do you propose?" Fox asked.

"Let's get back home," said Salter.

A murmur went around the room. Fox shook his head and turned to Kennedy. "Let's see that city."

Once again the camera's eye carried them along, higher and higher into the rugged mountains. Presently a pass appeared, and the ship skimmed through, barely clearing the crags as it slid down into the valley below. Bob Kennedy sat forward eagerly. "You'll see it now—it was right down—"

His voice faded as they stared at the films. A ragged valley floor, passing swiftly beneath them, a break in the clouds, a view of more mountains in the distance.

There was no sign of any city.

They watched to the end of the film. "Is there any more?" Kennedy asked sharply. "Any film that didn't come out?"

"Not a bit," said Fox. "This is it, all of it."

"Let me see it again."

Once again they watched. Commander Fox took a deep breath. "I don't see anything here that looks like a city."

"Neither do I," Kennedy said bleakly. He was silent for a long moment, staring at the screen. "Commander, *it was there*. I *know* it was there."

"Buildings?"

"Towers, spires, streets—I saw them." The photographer twisted uncomfortably. "I couldn't be wrong, either. It was like no city I've ever seen before. I'd swear it was nothing that was ever built by human hands."

Commander Fox's eyes were very bright. He walked to the observation screen and stared down at the gray expanse of planet that lay below as the men watched him and waited. Finally he turned, rubbing his palms together. "Mr. Morehouse, take the ship down."

"On the delta?"

"If that's the safest place to drop it."

"It's the only place," said Kennedy.

"Fine," said the Commander. "Put it down there, then. We're going to have a look at that ship on the ridge. We're going to have a look at that city, too—or whatever else it may be."

Three hours later Morehouse had demonstrated his qualifications as a Star Ship navigator by making a near-impossible landing without so much as a jar on touching down. The job had been done virtually blind, for as the *Ganymede* settled toward the planet's surface the clouds also had descended, and the ship touched down in a violent torrent of freezing wind and rain. Crewmen at the observation ports gave up their watch in short order; there was nothing to see but the black muddy ground around the ship, and the blanket of gray that swallowed it up on all sides.

They waited, breathlessly, for something to happen. Nothing did. The wind howled and died, the fog closed in closer, but that was all. Soon the grayness turned to blackness, and they knew that night had come.

Meanwhile, the crew were at work preparing gear and supplies for the landing parties. "I want six men on the ship at all times," Commander Fox told them. "Dorffman, you'll be at the radio to keep in contact with both parties, and to warn the others if there is any irregularity. Our first job will be a preliminary look around, primarily to determine the best route up to that wrecked ship. You can keep Mangano and Morehouse with you, and three others."

"Both parties?" Dorffman asked.

"Yes. The rest of us will split into groups of eight, and move out separately. Lorry, you'll be in charge of one; I'll lead the other, and we'll move in opposite directions from the ship, heading for the mountain range. You take Kennedy with you; I'll take Lambert. We'll want to move by daylight, if nothing turns up during the night to change our minds, so you'd better get things set up. We'll only be out over one night for the first recon, so we shouldn't need the half-tracks. We may find them useful the second time out if we decide to make an overland try for the wrecked ship."

Peter Brigham had been busy in the navigation shack ever since Kennedy had returned with his films and his odd story of the "city" in the valley. When he finally got back to the bunkroom he found Lars poring over a checklist of supplies. "Well! What did *you* think of Kennedy's story?" he asked Lars as he flopped down on the bunk.

Lars shrugged. "Not very much to think."

"But he didn't make sense!" Peter exclaimed. "He says he saw a city, sort of. Only it wasn't on the film. Not a sign of it."

Lars nodded. As he had watched the films he had had the same queer sensation of dread and wonder that he had felt the day Commander Fox had revealed the true mission of the *Ganymede*. "Obviously he either saw something that the camera didn't pick up, or else he only thought he saw something."

Peter grinned excitedly. "But what about the *Planetfall?* You saw the films. Did that look like the kind of a crackup that anyone could have lived through?"

Lars hesitated. "No—"

"You bet it didn't. And yet there were messages broadcast from here *after* the *Planetfall* landed, remember? So the messages that were received must either have been sent before the ship landed, or else they weren't sent by the crew of the *Planetfall* at all."

Lars put his list down and stared at Peter. "I hadn't thought of that."

"Well, think about it for a minute."

"What are you trying to say?"

"Just that there's something very strange going on. I don't know what, exactly, but something. You start thinking about it, and nothing quite fits. Know what I mean? You look at it briefly and everything seems perfectly obvious. The *Planetfall* landed on Wolf IV, the crew radioed its landing home, started to explore their landing, and were overwhelmed by some sort of alien force or other. Now, if you assume that there *are* aliens here, it seems to tie up into a nice, neat bundle, *until you start to examine it closely.* And then, all of a sudden, it falls apart, because the parts just don't add up right."

Lars shook his head. "I still don't see what you're driving at."

"It's hard to explain. Look, do you remember those abstract-recognition tests they used to give us back at the Academy? They flashed colored pictures on the screen for a tenth of a second and then asked us what we saw that was wrong? Most of the errors were simple—a man with a woman's hat on, or something like that—but then there was that series that almost everybody missed, remember?"

"You mean the ones where they'd omitted the processing for one of the colors?"

"That's right! Take a color picture of a mountain landscape, for instance, and just fail to process it for red. It looks awfully peculiar, but you're really up against it to say exactly *why.*" Peter jumped up excitedly. "That's what this whole business looks like to me—a color picture with one of the colors missing. Some big factor, influencing everything that's happened, that we just can't even see. Something we're missing entirely."

"Of course, it could be the nature of the aliens themselves," Lars suggested.

"Maybe. But I'm not so sure it has anything to do with aliens. That's another thing. If there are aliens here, where are they? They certainly haven't come rushing out to greet us. But I think the thing we're missing is something different, and I don't think we're going to nail it down until we get close enough to the wreck of the *Planetfall* to see just exactly what *did* happen to her."

"Which crew are you going with?" Lars asked.

"I don't know. Have they been assigned?"

"I'm assigned to go with Fox and Lambert," said Lars. "You'd better check. We ought to try to be together."

"We will," said Peter. "If I have to beat old Foxy over the head with his own log book."

Preparations were nearly completed when John Lambert conferred with Fox in the control room an hour or so before dawn.

"Supplies should be adequate for forty-eight hours, but thirty-six would be safer to plan on," he told the Commander, a worried frown on his face.

"The heater-packs are charged on the suits?"

"Oh, yes. We'll be warm enough. On a longer trek we'd have to carry generators for recharges, but this will do for a preliminary reconnaissance. The other things, too, auxiliary oxygen, though we shouldn't need it. Medical supplies for emergencies—"

Fox frowned. "Then what's worrying you, John?"

Lambert sighed, and took a bucket seat across from the Commander. "I don't know. Nothing important."

"If something's bothering you, it's important," Fox said. "I know that by now. Come on, man. Out with it."

Lambert looked at him. "Walter, are you sure this is smart? Taking so many men off the ship at once?"

"You thinking of an attack?"

"Well—vaguely."

"If they were going to attack us, they've had plenty of

time. We were in orbit for over a week, and nothing came up to scrap with us. We've been down now for twenty-four hours, and not a peep."

"I'd still feel better with just one crew out."

Fox chewed his lip. "You meant the talking that's going on."

"Partly. It isn't in the open like it was before, but it's there. And I don't think that Peter Brigham has anything to do with it this time. But it's an ugly undercurrent just the same. I'm worried that something is going to break wide open."

Walter Fox stared out the observation port, his hands clenched behind his back as he watched the slow orange-gray light spreading across the land. The fog had lifted; he could see the river now, and the mountains very close. He turned back to Lambert, shaking his head. "You weren't with me when we ran up against the dust-devils on Arcturus IV, were you? No, that was before your time. Ten, eleven years ago. We thought they were intelligent aliens, at first. No, they weren't legends, they existed. And we know now that there was no intelligence, as we know it, in them; just a hungry, malignant, instinctive urge to destruction. They killed by means of the violent waves of fear they could drive through men's minds, blind, raging fear. They would have wiped out my crew if I'd let them sit there and wait for the creatures to come. But I didn't do that. I got them on their feet and made them march. I shouted at them, and whipped them, and drove them."

Fox rubbed a hand across his eyes, as though the memory even now was cruel. "I made those men hate me with all the bitterness they could muster, because by hating me they could keep alive, and by giving way to fear they would have died. I killed three of them, just as surely as if

I'd run knives into their throats, but I brought nineteen back safely and broke a planet that now gives homes to seven million Earthmen."

He paused, looking down at Lambert. "You don't finish paying a price like that for a planet very soon, John. You keep paying it over and over again. But you learn some things. I've learned enough to know that my men have to move into the teeth of this thing, whatever it is, that's waiting for us. It's here, I'm certain of it. And it's waiting."

Lambert still looked unhappy, and the Commander smiled. "Stop worrying," he said. "We won't move fast, or very far, until we see what things are like out there. It's just a step outside to look around. But we can't wait for—whatever it is—to move first. We've waited as long as we dare."

"Well, maybe you're right," Lambert said finally. "I won't mind getting out and stretching my legs a bit. I understand Lars will be with us, and Salter. Who else?"

"Leeds, Carstairs and Klein. And there may be another. If you're going below, tell Peter Brigham I'd like to see him."

Peter had not found his name on either landing party roster, and was somewhat startled at the Commander's early morning summons. He found Fox alone in the control room, staring gloomily out at the frozen land around the ship. A dozen protests were in Peter's mind as he stepped into the room, but when he was face to face with Fox, they suddenly faded in confusion, and he felt a flush of shame.

He really didn't have any grounds to demand very much, he reflected.

"Mr. Morehouse has given me a good report on your

work in his department, Brigham," Fox began. "An excellent report, in fact. He thinks that with time and experience you could make a top-rate navigator. That's quite a compliment from Morehouse, I might add, and he's not given to compliments."

"I—I'm glad he's satisfied," Peter stammered.

"Yes," said Fox. "So am I. But now we've got the problem of landing parties to face, and landing parties are a little different from the normal routine on a Star Ship."

"Yes, sir," said Peter tightly.

"I think maybe it's time we understood each other. I understand perfectly well the part you were playing early on this trip to turn the men against me. You know that, but you may not know that I also know why."

Peter's face was pale. "Then you know—"

"I know that you are your father's son, yes. I've known what you have been doing for quite a number of years, you see. I've known that one time or another we were going to have to face things out. We can never break free of the past, and we never make decisions that are universally good. I owed you this voyage, and I hoped that out of it you might grow to understand what happened to your father so long ago. I hoped you might even understand why my decision was *right,* even though it killed Thomas Brigham. But be that as it may, I do know that I can't in clear conscience order you to join a landing party here. You may go, or stay on the ship, as you choose."

Peter stared at him for a long moment. "Lars is going with you?" he asked finally.

"Yes."

"Then I want to go."

"You understand that we can't have any fun and games.

I've got to have a hundred per cent support. If you have any doubts about that, I warn you: stay on the ship."

"I want to go." There was no hesitation in Peter's voice. Commander Fox nodded, and offered his hand. Peter took it.

An hour later, the first landing party moved through the lock and stepped down to the surface of Wolf IV.

8

THE FOULEST BLOW

THEY STOOD on a cold and gloomy land. An icy wind whipped down the valley that the river cut in the mountain rim and howled like demons in their ears. They were not cold; the bulky heater-suits with their power-packs strapped on their backs kept arms and faces warm enough, filtered and warmed the thin oxygen atmosphere before it struck their nostrils. But the heater-suits could not begin to keep out the desolation and coldness that spread around them and chilled them far deeper than their bones.

Lars had heard of the feeling. The old-timers called it "land-shock" and it struck Lars like a tidal wave as he felt frozen mud crunch under his boots. Until this moment he had been protected, warm and secure in the bosom of a ship that was, in effect, an extension of home. Hull plates were thin, and the shell of the ship was frail enough, but its strength lay in what it represented. Now that strength was sheared away, and he felt for the first time the desolation of no protection, the almost physical shock of standing alone, a frail flesh and blood creature, on the open surface of a barren, alien land. There was a sense of loss, of overpowering dread, and Lars found a dozen panicky thoughts flooding his mind as he glanced over his shoulder at the ship behind them: *Suppose it's gone when we come back. What if we were stranded here, without ship, without food? What if—they—attacked while we were gone? What if—*

He thrust the thoughts angrily from his mind, even as a shiver went through him. The groups of men were huddled around Commander Fox now as he gave them their last briefing. Lars moved into the huddle, heard the Commander's voice, metallic through the speaker-plate of his suit.

"Now this is a routine reconnaissance, nothing more. We aren't aiming to go far from the ship, nor to do too much on this trip, just a standard look around. Got that? We've got two major objectives: to confirm our preliminary findings of surface conditions, soil, atmosphere, any indigenous plant or animal life; and to see if it's practical to try to take our half-track crawlers up that mountainside to the wrecked ship. Mr. Lorry, you'll take your men and try to find a way across the river on your side, then check for an approach from the right. I'll take my men and do the same on the left. We'll make hourly checks with each other, and with the ship. Got that?"

"Lorry nodded. "What about encampment?"

"We'll have a short day, so it will be best to find a good encampment place, and return back to the ship tomorrow. You can break in any newcomers to outpost camping techniques, and get them trained for an assault on the wreck later. Kennedy, keep an eye on the terrain—I'll want your opinion on the best approach to that thing up there—whether you can drop men from the scooter and pick them up again, or whether you can bring the scooter in to land somewhere higher than this. Okay? Let's go!"

The Commander's group began assembling. Salter and Leeds were huddled to one side with Bob Tenebreck of Lorry's crew, talking rapidly and quietly, but the Commander was concerned with a final check of equipment and did not notice the hasty conference. Lars could not find Peter, at first; then he felt a hand on his shoulder, and they checked each other's packs. But Peter was watching the conference closely, and when it broke up he moved in beside Leeds as Lambert came up to join Lars.

They started across the frozen delta land, in pairs, with Commander Fox in the lead, carrying the light intercom equipment as they moved.

"Cold!" Lars said between his teeth as Lambert joined him.

"You feel it?"

"Just inside."

"I know. When I took my first step off a ship onto a new planet, I thought I was dead for sure." Lambert grinned. "You feel as if you're leaving your last hope of protection behind you."

"But *this* place—"

"You'll get over it. You'll be calling this 'home' in no time."

Lars grunted and bent against the stiff gale coming down the valley. The clouds were breaking to the sun-side now, flooding the frozen tundra with an unspeakably gloomy orange-gray light. "That I've got to see," he said. "Right now, the sooner we're back snug in the *Ganymede* the better I'll like it."

They were making their way across a hard, frozen stubble. Occasionally they broke through the icy crust, sinking ankle-deep into clinging brown mud. Ahead they could see the line of scrub trees clinging to the river's edge, and beyond the green-black line of the jungle's edge.

"I wonder why there's no vegetation here?" Lars puzzled.

"This probably floods every spring," Lambert said. "This is a poor excuse for summertime, but that's what it is. This will probably melt during the day and turn into a real quagmire. And there can't be much topsoil up there in those mountains to catch the runoff of snow, so it will fill the river during relatively warm summer days and cover these flats with mud." He blinked as a flight of small black birds went by them at rocket-like speed. "Looked like ducks, for a minute."

"They were," Lars said. "About the size of robins, though. And I bet they'd be tough to eat."

As they approached the river they found a surprising variety of animal life scuttling away at their approach. Most of the creatures were gray or black, with nature's universal color protection, blending perfectly into the tarn. The sun rose higher, until the men cast shadows, but presently the sunlight flickered as deeper shadows crossed it.

Fox signaled a halt, and all eight men blinked up at the sky. Two mammoth hawk-like creatures were gliding across the cloud-studded sky, circling, returning. Hardly a feather fluttered in their wings, which seemed to form a black cape about their bodies. Suddenly the wings collapsed, and the creatures hurtled downward in perfect timing. A startled animal scream burst out near the landing party, and they heard the birds' wings crash open with a sound like muffled thunder as they rose again into the air. One of them gripped in its talons a tiny furry creature like a short-eared rabbit and tried to make off with its prey, but the others moved in to battle. In an instant the sky was full of feathers of the great hawks and they screamed and raked each other, the rabbit falling to the ground forgotten.

They moved on toward the river, loading their sample bags with bits of the scrub vegetation and samples of soil and rock. Tiny insects scurried out of their way. "How can they live in this climate?" Commander Fox asked, dropping back to confer with Lambert.

"Probably genetic adaptability," Lambert replied. "We saw the same thing in the microscopic flora. We can assume that this planet was not always so cold and that the change came gradually. Possibly it is having an ice age, just as we know happened on Earth. I want to see those trees, though. I'll bet they're tough little plants!"

"Shouldn't be long now. The river's right ahead."

They didn't hurry. They paused for hourly checks with Lorry's crew, matching their progress toward the other side of the delta. As they moved, the mountains ahead loomed bigger and more formidable. But nowhere was there any sign of life other than the simple forms they saw around them.

At last they reached the river, a wild, gray turbulent stream three hundred yards wide, throwing up a roar of sound that all but drowned out their voices. They moved up the banks, looking for a more favorable crossing place, and Fox signaled to stop for some lunch. It was as Lars sank down to munch his share of the self-heating ration that he made the first discovery.

Later they debated loudly what it was doing there, how it had gotten there, what its presence signified, but at the moment it was the source of unreasonable excitement, for beyond doubt it was a link, an artifact of home, of Earth, or Earthmen.

Lars thought it was a stone, at first, when he sat opposite it and blinked at it vacantly while he ate. His thoughts were far afield, and he must have stared at it for full five minutes before his mind gripped what his eyes were seeing: a gray speckled stone with the dim letters *SS Planetfall* spread across it.

He let out a cry, dropping his rations into the mud. He stared harder, and saw it was a bag, a standard gray canvas food bag, lying half-buried in the mud near the river's edge. The rest of the men gathered around, and they pulled it open, revealing half a dozen un-opened rations cans, three cans opened and empty, a tiny medical pack, a formless paper folder that could have been nothing but cigarets at some time in the past.

"But how did it get here?" Jerry Klein, the little brown-eyed meteorologist wanted to know.

"If this river floods, it might have come from anywhere upstream from here," Lambert suggested excitedly. "Could they have come down from the wreck, do you think? Made camp here, or near here?"

They scattered along the river bank, searching for other artifacts, but found nothing. "Lots more likely that it was washed down from the wreck itself," Salter said gloomily. "Just one more reason to think that they're all dead."

"With three opened cans? They wouldn't have opened rations unless they were landed from the ship," Lars countered.

"All right, then they were attacked," Salter growled. "I can't see what difference it makes."

But it did make a difference, a very real difference. Here was evidence that could not be ignored that the *Planetfall* had made a landing on Wolf IV. But a safe landing? The food bag only made the question the more confusing.

At any rate, they were on their feet again, anxious to be on. Once again Peter teamed with Leeds. They seemed to be talking a great deal. Only once could Lars catch Peter's eye, as they moved on up the river bank, and when he did, he felt a shiver go up his spine. It was only a glance, but there was an almost eerie quality of appeal in it. It was as though Peter were trying, desperately, to tell him something without words or signs. Yet when Lars paused to come closer Peter shook his head angrily and motioned him curtly away.

Lambert saw Lars' puzzled frown. "What's up?"

Lars hesitated, then shook his head. "Nothing."

Lambert grunted skeptically, but moved ahead with him. At last they reached a place where the river was broader, but seemed less turbulent. Fox motioned them together. "I want to try to get across, if we can. It looks like some sort of trail along the far side. There might be a better view up the mountains from there. Think we can manage with the rafts?"

Lars stared at the waterway. "I think I could paddle across with a line. Then it would be easy to ferry across, and we could leave the rafts there to return with."

"Want to give it a try? We'll have you secure with a line from this side."

It was not too difficult. They inflated the rafts with CO_2 cartridges, and loaded Lars' pack into another raft. Lars secured the coil of nylon cord to his waist, and pushed the rubber boat out into the stream. He paddled swiftly, not trying to fight the current but allowing it to help him. Slowly the far bank became more distinct, until he found a landing spot, and began moving upstream to the point opposite the party. Fifteen minutes later the line was taut to a gnarled scrub tree, and the party pulled themselves across in the rafts.

Now they were in the jungle, if it could be called that. The trees were twisted and short, with iron-hard branches and little clumps of needle-like leaves. They stood like gnarled skeletons, their branches interlacing into an impenetrable thicket, but they did not break the wind which whistled through them. Across the river the ship was gone from sight, hidden by the trees and the inevitable mist that settled. But here they found a trail moving up into higher ground, toward the mountains. Fox led the way forward without a pause after cacheing the rafts securely among the trees.

At the top of the rise the mountains were clearly in view, outlined in the now fading daylight. Fox studied them closely with his field glasses for a long time. Then he grunted and handed the glasses to Klein. "See what you can see."

The meteorologist studied the rising bastion. "Rough," he said at last. "I thought I caught a glimpse of the ship, but then the clouds came down."

"It's there. But getting to it is another thing."

"Let me have a look." Lambert took the glasses. "From here, I doubt if we could get a crawler up there. But that ridge up ahead hides the view. Maybe from there we could see a way."

Jeff Salter took the glasses. "Why not move up there tomorrow?" he said. "We'd have better light."

"No place to encamp here," Lambert said. "But we could see better, that's true."

"We'll go on a mile or so farther," Fox decided at last. "At least we may find a better camping spot."

They moved out again. Here, in the forest and with gathering darkness they did not have the visibility they had on the delta. Everyone was jittery. Lars felt time and again for the bulge of his machine pistol against his leg as he watched the shadowy darkness creep in. But finally they found an open place, level, but with some protection afforded by an outcropping of rock. Here they set up the insulated shelter tents, huddling in against the rocks for safety from the wind. Fox checked with Lorry, and shook his head unhappily.

"Lorry doesn't see any approach from his side. A solid cliff runs along the bottom. He's planning to go back to the ship at daylight."

"What about us?" Peter asked.

"We'll scout ahead to see if there's a break in the ridge on our side. If there's not, it'll be up to Kennedy to drop someone up there, or else we'll have to figure another approach. But we've got to get up there."

Several of the men went out for scrap wood to build a watch fire. They did not need the heat, and the food was self-heated, but no one argued against a fire. The thought of spending a night out on this desolate place without a cheering blaze to watch by was not pleasant. But getting a fire was another thing. The wood refused to burn. It took an hour of wittling and coaxing to start a small blaze, and then it flickered and smoked, anything but cheerful.

They ate in silence. Everyone was weary from the trek. Lambert checked his pedometer and announced that they had made approximately eight miles. It had felt like fifty. Lars was quite satisfied to be assigned to late watch, allowing him some sleep first. Fox and Klein took the first watch; Peter and Leeds were assigned to the second. Peter was to waken Lars and Lambert to cover the third period, while Salter and Carstairs would cover the pre-dawn hours. They all checked their pistols. "Keep the fire going," Lars admonished, and crawled into his tent, setting his heater-suit at sleeping temperature. Lambert stayed outside to talk with Fox and Klein for a while; Lars was still awake when he finally came to bed.

"What's the trouble, insomnia?"

"No, just too much to think about." Lars turned over restlessly. Certainly there had been no sign of an alien intelligence at work on this planet, so far, and yet the threat still hung heavily. It took a long while for Lars to relax, but at last he slept heavily. Outside the clouds closed in to obscure the stars in blackness.

Lars awoke suddenly, his whole body tense. Something was wrong. There had been no sound, yet he felt danger screaming in his ears. What? *What had happened?* He tried to see, peering across toward Lambert, snoring, and felt the hair rise along the ridge of his spine.

The fire. He had gone to sleep with a yellow-red reflection flickering on the tent flaps.

It was gone now. Instead there was only a dull red glow.

He knew he had been sleeping a long time, too long! Peter had not awakened him for his watch. He fumbled for his wrist-light, flashed it on his chronometer, trying to shake himself awake. Six hours!

He pulled himself to the opening of the tent, peered out. There was deathly silence. Not even the wind howled now. A pile of half-dead embers glowed redly where the fire had been.

With a cry Lars burst from the tent, staring about for the men on watch, machine pistol on ready in his hand. There was no sign of the guard. The pack-sacks, neatly piled near the rock, were torn open, their contents scattered wildly.

Others began burrowing out of their tents now—Lambert, his eyes wide with alarm; Klein, stumbling like a drunken man as he pitched toward the fire, staring in dismay; Fox, his face grim. "What happened? What's wrong?" somebody shouted.

They stood staring at the rifled packs, and blinking at each other, as realization flooded their faces.

"Gone!" Lambert said bleakly.

"They can't be gone!" Lars protested. He ran to the other tents, flashed his light inside. Nobody there. "They can't be. Peter wouldn't have gone without—" He stopped short, shaking his head.

Peter *was* gone. So were Salter, Leeds and Carstairs. Lars remembered the hurried conference, Peter's teaming with Leeds during the day, the quiet talking. Suddenly everything fell into a pattern.

"They're gone, all right," Fox said heavily. "Run out on us like—"

"But where?"

"Where do you suppose? Back to the ship, of course. Where's that talker—if I can get Dorffman before—"

"You won't use this talker," Klein said quietly, pointing to a pile of junk tossed in the mud nearby. "They've taken care of that. They've got the food, too, or most of it. Look at that mess."

"They can't get across the river," Lars said suddenly. Then he remembered the rafts by the shore.

"They not only have the rafts, they have the line to ferry across with." Fox's face was grim. "Klein, we've got to try to stop them. It looks like they have an hour's start, at least."

"Why try?" Klein asked. "Won't the men at the ship stop them when they see we're not with them?"

"I don't think so. I think this has been planned for some time. I'm sorry, Lars, but it *must* have been. If Lorry has had a run-out too, there would be enough of them to take the ship. We've got to stop them. If we don't there may not be any ship when we get back there."

He and Klein checked their guns. "Lambert, you and Lars stick here. See if there's any chance of getting that talker working. The river will delay them, and we may be able to stop them there." With that the two men started down the trail toward the river again.

Lars piled the fire high, avoiding Dr. Lambert's eyes as he worked to make order of the rifled packs. High above the clouds were gone, and stars shone like cold, unwinking eyes. It was colder now, and Lars turned up his heater control.

"Better spare that," Lambert said quietly. "We may need it badly."

"You don't think they'd—"

"I don't know what to think. They've run for it, that's all. They must have been planning for weeks to grab their first chance, and this was it."

"Peter Brigham hasn't been in on anything like that," Lars protested. "He *couldn't* have been."

"I'm afraid the facts don't bear you out," said Lambert. "I'm sorry. But I don't see any other explanation. He must have known what was up, and yet he gave no warning."

They sat about the fire, waiting as a half hour passed, then an hour. A gray dawn was creeping up the horizon as they peered anxiously in the direction of the ship. "You—you think they'll blast if they get to the ship and take it?" Lars asked.

"I'm afraid so."

"But that would leave us—"

"Yes. It would leave us in trouble, bad trouble." Lambert's lips were a grim line. "Keep watching. We'll see the blast from here."

They watched, expecting momentarily to see the bright orange-red jet trail suddenly rise into the sky. But there was no sign. At last they heard noises down the trail, and Fox and Klein sat wearily down by the fire. Defeat was written in heavy lines across their faces. "You saw it, I suppose," Fox said lifelessly.

"Saw it?" Lambert frowned.

"The blast-off. You must have seen it from up here."

"We didn't see any blast-off," Lars said stolidly. "We've been watching."

Fox and Klein exchanged puzzled glances. "That's odd," said Fox. "We followed them, and dragged ourselves across the river on the line, they'd conveniently cut loose the rafts. We followed their trail clear across the delta to the place where the ship had been. They must have been successful, taken Dorffman and the others by surprise."

"Look," said Lars. "That ship never blasted, with Salter and his crowd in charge of it, or anybody else."

"It must have," Commander Fox said grimly. "Because it's gone. *There isn't any ship on the delta where we set her down*. There's *nothing* out there." He looked intently at Lars and Lambert and Klein. "And you know what that means. That means we're stranded here. It means we've got to reach that ship up there on the ridge, and reach her fast if we don't want to starve to death."

9

THE THING ON THE RIDGE

IT TOOK Lars several moments fully to realize the enormity of what Commander Fox was saying. The *Ganymede* was gone. They had not seen it go, nor heard it go, but it was gone nevertheless. Like the silent deserters who had rifled the packs and departed during the night, the ship had suddenly and incredibly vanished. They were alone—Fox, Jerry Klein, John Lambert, and himself. They had power for their heater-suits for another twenty-eight hours, perhaps; at best there could be only food enough for two days left in the packs. Beyond that, nothing.

"What about Lorry and his group?" Lambert was asking quietly.

"No sign of them. They may still be sleeping, for all I know."

"Shouldn't we try to contact them?"

"It would mean crossing the river at least once, and then crossing back," Fox said slowly. "It would mean losing heat and using up an extra day's food. Assuming that they're alive, that is. No, we're going to need that heat and food ourselves, John. We can only hope and pray that there's more food up there—" he glanced up the black cliffs of the ridge—"where the bag we found came from. I don't think we'd survive very long trying to live off the land."

"At least we could give them a burst of gunfire," Klein offered. "Then they'd know we were still alive.

"We could try it," Fox said cautiously. "Just a short round, though. We may need the ammunition."

Klein lifted his machine pistol and fired a rapid volley. The sharp crack-crack-crack echoed and re-echoed down the valley, as they stood waiting, listening for a return.

Nothing. Silence, except for the rising wind.

"They'll go the same way we're going," Fox said finally. "There's only one way *to* go, and that's up. We'd better get going."

His voice was lifeless, but his eyes glinted with anger. Quickly they checked the gear that remained. Lars' estimate of two days' food was optimistic: there were two meals apiece for them, not counting the few cans in the *Planetfall* bag they had discovered. They opened the first of the cans now, and ate with a pretense of heartiness that none of them felt. Lambert found his medical pack intact, and handed around stress-caps. "Any idea how long it'll take us to get up there?"

"Too long," Fox growled.

"Well, these will be good protection if we don't have to depend on them too heavily."

"I still don't see why we didn't see the ship blast," Lars

said. "Could they have thrown it straight into Koenig drive without clearing the planet?"

"If they did, we're better off than they are, because they'd all be dead. They'd have disintegrated half the planet and blown themselves to atoms. No, Salter was a navigator. He knows you have to be in free space to use the drive."

"I still don't see how they could have blasted," Lars said doggedly.

"Do you want to go back there and look for yourself?" Fox snapped. "Do you think I'm blind? Or are you just so sold on your friend that you can't admit to yourself that he's turned traitor? Eh? Well?"

"There's no point to fighting about it," Lambert cut in. "It's not there. All right. That cuts it pretty thin for us. We'd better make the best of what we've got."

Fox glowered at Lars for a moment; then his face softened. "John's right," he said. "Sorry. I guess I just needed something to strike out at. Have we got those packs ready? Let's move."

They moved. They had no enthusiasm for it, but they realized that now was the time to make speed, while they had warmth and food. The started up the trail toward the jutting ridge, Fox and Klein leading, Lars and Lambert behind. The wind was high now, bearing down on them as though to hinder progress as much as it could, and angry black clouds scudded across the bleak sky.

"How long can a man go without food?" Lars asked Lambert as they worked their way up the rocky animal trail.

"With plenty of water, quite a while. Provided he doesn't have to use up his energy moving, and provided he has no coldness and wetness to worry about. It isn't food we have to worry about for a while yet. If you want to fret about something, fret about pneumonia, or broken legs."

The latter, at least, was an ever present danger. The tough underbrush covered the trail, giving way from time to time to piles of broken rock, the remains of ancient slides. Soon the trail took a sharp upward course as they moved around the face of the ridge they had seen the night before, blanking out their view of the mountain ridge beyond. What if they, too, found blank cliff waiting for them around the abutment? Lars felt his slender nylon cord looped around his shoulder. It was strong, but one man had to get up a cliff before others could climb a rope.

It took several hours of work to reach the end of the obstruction, but finally they broke out on a high rounded knoll and could see the rising crags before them. The cliff extended up from the far side of the river, where the stream of water coursed over it in a gigantic waterfall. But here there was a break in the obstructing wall. A jagged slide-course of boulders slanted up through a split in the cliff, reaching to a snow-covered plateau above. Far above this, as the clouds broke, they caught a glint of metal.

"It's bad," Fox said. "It'll take a day at least to get up that slide, if we can do it without breaking our necks. And then I'm not certain we can get onto those higher ridges that lead to the ship."

Jerry Klein studied the course with field glasses. "I've done some climbing back home," he said. "It looks possible—barely—from here. Of course, I don't know what it'll look like from there."

"I wish we had Kennedy's films," Fox said.

"They wouldn't help much. It isn't the horizontal plane that worries me, it's the vertical. That's a vicious rise there."

"But it looks possible?"

"I think so."

"Then let's move," said Commander Fox.

They did not reach the top of the rock-slide by darkness. The day was spent scrambling over boulders the size of a house, working their way like a creeping snake up the treacherous mountainside. In full daylight it was difficult enough; when darkness fell Fox shook his head bitterly and waved the others in to a small cul-de-sac in the rock. "We'll have to stop here. Let's have a little food."

They were exhausted and ravenous. They took half-rations, and felt as though they had eaten nothing. Then they tried to find comfortable places to sleep. It was hopeless. Lars dozed, jerking awake a dozen times as the hard rocks pushed through his heater-suit. About midnight it began to snow, huge white flakes piling up on the dozing men, drifting against the rocks. Then Lars awoke to find his hands and toes numb with cold, and knew that his heater-pack was exhausted.

By daylight they were all cold. The food warmed them a little, but it was nearly the last, and it was not enough. They stomped themselves warm in the snow, and peered up into the blustery grayness that lay above them.

"Let's move," said Fox. They moved.

With aching limbs they started on up the slide. The ventilated suits were a burden now, insulating them somewhat, but growing too warm as they climbed, chilling them to the bone when they stopped. The whiteness around them grew thicker as they climbed, but Lars paid no attention to the surroundings. He kept his eyes on Jerry Klein's boots above him, and followed, step by step upward, as the trip began to dissolve into a series of nightmare impressions, fleeting thoughts, almost-hopeless hopes.

Movement—to keep warm, to keep moving. Upward,

always upward. A pause after what seemed like days, to finish the rations, melt some of the snow for water. Then on again. One foot forward, then the other. A scramble, a shout, a flurry of snow as Fox lost his footing, starting a small slide down toward them, and then the pause to rope together. Another pause, as they reached the top of the slide, searched the crags above for a way to reach further up. Darkness, and coldness, another dawn. Above them, the mountain like a living, malignant thing, daring them to keep coming, but high on a ridge near the summit, a glint of metal, a glint of hope.

They moved upward.

It was too easy to despair. Lars found himself thinking bleakly of the wreck high above them on the ridge. Would they find food there? Would the generators still work, would there be recharges for their heater-packs? There had to be, if they hoped to survive. But there was more up there, more waiting for them. For the hundredth time Lars remembered Peter Brigham's words: *It just doesn't fit, any of it. And we won't nail it until we reach that wreck and find out what really happened to the* Planetfall.

And over it all, the growing conviction that they were not alone on this planet, somehow, that somewhere alien eyes were watching, waiting.

On the fourth day they met the remainder of Lorry's group.

It was a sorry reunion. They met on a high ridge, where Fox and his group had fought for hours to climb a series of rocky abutments. Tom Lorry spotted them from the other side of the ridge and shouted; then he was running toward them, with Bob Kennedy at his heels. Behind came Marstom, the engineer. There were no others.

"Where are the rest?" Fox demanded when they had joined into a huddled group on the ridge.

"Three of them ran out," Lorry panted. "We all started up when we found the ship gone, but Blair broke his ankle. I left him down below with Burger and all the food we had. They've got fuel, and some protection from the wind. We started on up then. How is your food supply?"

"It isn't," Fox said.

"Then let's get going. There's got to be food in that wreck."

They moved upward.

That night Kennedy began coughing, and so did Marstom. By morning both were feverish. Fox and Lars had frostbitten fingers which Lambert nursed back to warmth again. The wind was back, cold and biting, carrying drifts of sleet down the mountainside upon them. Lambert loaded both men with antibiotic, and distributed the rest of his stress-caps. They had lost sight of the wreck above them now; they were too close against the mountainside. But Klein thought he saw a way up.

"We can't take these men with fevers," Lambert protested.

"We can't leave them here. Maybe there'll be some shelter when we get up there, some food."

Both men agreed. Marstom had difficulty with his breathing as they started to hike again, but by stopping periodically he was able to keep up. Kennedy was wracked with coughing. They moved up one cliff face, then another. Only once that day did they see their goal. It looked as distant as the day they had started. But they knew it couldn't be. "Another push, a hard one, tomorrow and we might make it," Fox said hopefully. "We'll have to start as soon as there's any light at all. How are the sick ones?"

"I'm nearly out of drugs," Lambert said.

"But they're holding their own?"

"For now."

"There may be drugs on the ship."

"If there's just some food it'll suit me," Jerry Klein growled. "There might even be some way to salvage it, you know."

"Of course!" Fox said, forcing enthusiasm. "If only the engines are reparable, it wouldn't be tough to repair a wrecked shell. But we can't do it down here. Let's try to sleep now, and then move. I don't want to spend another night on this iceberg with a rock for a pillow."

"It'll be a tough climb tomorrow," Klein warned.

"So we climb," said Fox. "At least we'll stay warm that way."

That night Lars began coughing, felt the unnatural heat of fever in his cheeks. By the time light was visible, he felt groggy, stumbling forward with the others in a dim half-world of unreality. He was tired, tired beyond words, tired with a bone-weariness that cut all purpose out of his steps, as he fell mechanically into his place in line. He didn't even mention the fever to Lambert, what was the use? The drugs were almost gone. It seemed as though he were wrapped in a cocoon, miles away from the rest of the group, looking down on them as they moved up the steep face of the mountain. He found himself chuckling to himself, and caught himself sharply, shaking his head to bring reality closer.

They moved at infinitesimal speed, but they moved. A series of rock wall jutted up above them, vanishing into snow-clouds. Jerry Klein studied the wall, then began shinning up, wedging his feet into crevasses, seeking hand-holds, the coil of nylon cord over his shoulder. He vanished into the gloom as the others waited, not talking, not even looking up—just waiting. Then they heard his call, as the nylon swished wetly down to them, and they pulled themselves up, one by one. Lambert strapped Kennedy and Marstom tightly to the rope, and Lars and Fox pulled from above to help them up. One such climb behind them, another loomed up, and another. With each passing moment Lars' hopes sank; he was moving in a dream now, hardly paying attention to anything. *It was a delusion all along*, he thought. *We shouldn't have hoped to make it*.

But always there was the flicker of hope, wan and fading, but present. They took the next rock wall, and steadied themselves for the next.

But there wasn't any next.

They were on a snowfield, a high narrow valley stretching up to the very summit of the mountain beyond. Clouds scudded across, blotting out the peak, then revealing it again, and the snow was a fuzzy blanket as it fell. Across the snowfield was a crag that wasn't a crag, but the jets of a Star Ship, dimly outlined, one fin raised in gray silhouette against the sky. A cry went up, and Fox and Lorry were running through waist-deep snow, fighting their way toward the distant outline. Lars stumbled after them as Kennedy and Marstom fell to their knees, then scrambled up again in their eagerness. A cloud blotted out the view, but they had seen it, *they knew it was there*. Half laughing, half crying, Lars stumbled after the dark figures of Fox and Lorry, leaving Lambert to catch up as he could.

Then, as if a signal had been given, the snow stopped and the obscuring cloud lifted. They were very near the wrecked ship now, near enough to see the detail, when Commander Fox stopped cold in his tracks, staring at her. Lorry stumbled, gripped Fox's shoulder, and pulled himself erect again, panting as he too stared. Something cold crept up Lars' spine; he stopped, blinking at the thing on the ridge ahead of him. It was a ship, a Star Ship, the goal they had fought so hard for.

But the ship didn't look right.

The lines were wrong, and it was too big. The part they could see rising up from the snowfield was not the full length of the hull, but only a fragment. It was a pile of wreckage, half-buried in silt and snow, disintegrating from the brutal weathering of many decades.

Lars rubbed his eyes, his mind denying what his eyes told him as he stumbled forward toward the wreck. It was an Earth ship—true—but it was *not* the *Star Ship Planetfall*. Barely legible letters on the windbeaten hull spelled out another name, the name of a ship that had left Earth over three hundred years before, taking its crew out bravely and blindly on the Long Passage.

The thing on the ridge was the wreck of the *Star Ship Argonaut*.

10

THE THING IN THE VALLEY

FOR AS much as five minutes they stood staring incredulously at the wraith before them, not moving, the only sound their panting breath. Snow began falling again, lazily, spinning down in their faces, falling to form yet another layer of snow on the ancient wreckage before them.

Then Jerry Klein burst forward with a sob. He tripped over a buried piece of hull plate, dragged himself to his feet and ran into the dead, swinging airlock door. He braced himself, peering in, and the door crashed off its hinges in his hands. *"Nothing!"* he cried. "There's nothing here. It's dead, *dead*."

He slammed the hull with his fist, and it jerked and swayed dangerously. As Fox and Lambert ran forward, Klein ducked into the gaping lock; they could hear him crashing about inside like a wild man.

And then they were all moving about the decaying ship, hoping against hope that their eyes had been playing tricks, searching for a sign of life, something to restore their hope. They moved through the twisted wreckage numbly, like ghosts of a time long past, searching for something they could no longer hope to find.

No food, no warmth. No hope of repairing engines smashed into fragments and buried under centuries of silt.

Nothing there but the half-buried skeleton of a ship long despaired of, almost forgotten.

They dragged Klein out of the wreckage laughing and giggling and screaming and fighting them with hysterical fury until Fox struck him hard across the face. He sagged, then, and crumpled into the snow, and sat staring dully at nothing and shaking his head.

When Fox turned to the others tears were streaming down his face. "Get those sick men on their feet, and get back on the rope again. We're going to go on."

Numbly, Lars and Lambert went back across the snow-field to the half-delirious Kennedy and Marstom. Their ship on the ridge had been a mirage, even worse than a mirage, for it had indeed existed, taunting them and drawing them on to the last moment. No one had dreamed that it could be the wrong ship. But now they knew that it was. Somehow, missing its course in that valiant journey so long ago, the *Argonaut* had found another star, another planet, and a grave. What had happened? How long had the journey taken? Only the decaying wreckage could hint at the answer.

The group of men who had labored up the mountain to find the lost *Planetfall* with its food and generators and its hope of escape from this gray death-planet had found a tomb instead.

They grouped around Walter Fox, Lars and Lambert supporting the sick men. Jerry Klein sat like a statue as a film of snow gathered on his arms and hands. Tom Lorry stood huddled near the wreckage, still staring, his face blank with exhaustion and despair.

"There's nothing here," Marstom said dully.

"No, there's not," Fox said.

"No food. No medicine."

"Nothing."

"No hope of salvaging this—" Marstom's lips curled bitterly "—this pile of trash."

"None."

"But there's got to be!" Marstom choked. "You said it was up here, the *Planetfall*. You said there'd be food, that we could get warm."

"This isn't the *Planetfall,*" Fox snapped. "We were wrong."

"You mean we were fools," Tom Lorry growled. "If this isn't the *Planetfall*, then *where is it?* We know it was here. You found the food bag. If it didn't crash here, what happened to it?"

"I don't know."

"Or our ship, what about it? Where did it go?"

"That's what we've got to find out," said Fox. "We'll never find out sitting here and freezing. We've got to move on."

"What's the use?" said Marstom. He broke into a paroxysm of coughing, his thin shoulders shaking. "This is as good a place to freeze as any."

"You've forgotten the thing in the valley," Fox said fiercely, "the thing Kennedy saw. The valley is just over the ridge here. Kennedy saw something."

"There's nothing there," Marstom snarled. "Kennedy

was sick, we've all been sick, crazy. There's nothing to go on for. This is the end right here."

"Get up," said Fox. "We're going up there. Get on your feet and get moving."

Nobody moved. Lars stared at the ground, his fingers numb, his whole body deathly tired. Marstom was right, something whispered in his ear. It was a lie, a delusion, that thing in the valley beyond the ridge. This was the end, right here.

And then, like a fury, Walter Fox was on his feet, cursing and shouting at them, his voice cutting like a whiplash, his face white, his eyes glittering like gray diamonds. "You idiots!" he shouted. "Are you going to just lie down and die?" He leaped on Jerry Klein, grabbed him by the collar and jerked him up to his feet. "Get up, do you hear me? *Up,* on your feet. You see the way up there, up over that saddle there—get going!" He gave Jerry a shove, and turned to jerk Tom Lorry's shoulder, dragging him by physical force as the second officer shook his head. "I'm in command here," Fox shouted, "and as long as I'm in command when I say we go on, we go on! You think you're just quitting on me? I'll drag you on my back first! Come on, *move*—nobody's ever quite a mission on *me* before, and you're not going to start a trend now!"

He whirled on Lars and Lambert. "What are you doing just standing there? Get those two men. Carry them, drag them, I don't care what, but get moving. We're going to find that ship if we have to walk every mile of this miserable planet."

Slowly, numbly, they began to move. Fox ran back and forth on the line, shouting at them, pounding them on the back, dragging Klein to his feet when he stumbled and pushing him forward again as they moved out and away from the wreck. Lars threw Kennedy's arm around his neck, half-supported the little man's body with his right arm, and they started forward. Every muscle in Lars' body ached, but the Commander's voice burned raw in his mind. He caught a bitter tongue-lashing as he paused to resettle his grip, and felt bitter anger flare, warming him, quickening his step. But mostly there was weariness, and wonder. How could Fox do it? How could he find this bottomless resource of burning energy, to drive and drive to the point of hopelessness, and then drive more? What miracle of strength and vitality could that man have? There were no answers, yet dimly a flicker of understanding flared in Lars' mind. *This was why he could lead, because he had strength where strength failed.*

They moved, a sorry beaten line, past the wrecked ship, on up the snowfield toward the low saddle of the pass before them. They didn't care what was beyond it now. All they cared was to get it over, to cross beyond, somehow. The wind was whipping the snow into a blizzard now, and darkness was falling rapidly; the rocks were becoming hazy and indistinct, even the expanse of white above and beyond grew gray, grayer. Lars stopped once and looked back, peering through the gloom to see the fantastic wreck they had left behind them, but he could see nothing but a wall of white.

Had it really been there? *Could* it have been there? Or had it been a feverish dream, a weird nightmare to torment them? Perhaps a vicious twist of their imaginations, a wraith, like the thing in the valley that Kennedy had thought he had seen. But it didn't matter now. All that mattered was one foot ahead, another, climb, stumble, climb some more, on up the ridge.

Until finally, imperceptibly in the darkness, they were moving *down* instead of up, and the ragged shadows of twisted trees were appearing below them, the timber line, high on this side of the pass, and the wind dying as they slid down into a protective cut in the rock and dragged wood up, wood that meant warmth at last, a place to rest in safety.

They were over the pass. Below them the valley lay, dark and imponderable before them.

Dawn came silent and windless and gray. The snow had stopped, and a wall of fog had descended, hiding all but the first lines of trees below the camping place. It was still cold, and there was no food, but the men felt at least half alive as light began to show grayly from over the pass.

They had thrown caution to the winds when they had reached that sheltering place, and built up a huge fire, warming themselves, drying their underclothes, drawing some element of life and hope from the yellow flames. And then they had slept, for the first time in days. Fox, Lorry, Lambert and Lars had split watches while the others slept like the rocks they were sleeping on. When Lars' turn came, he hardly felt the hard ground beneath him before he was in oblivion.

But with morning came some degree of orientation. They could not see the valley below them except for a few yards of gray slope downward because of the fog, but they knew that this was the valley where Kennedy had seen, or thought he had seen a city. A city that human hands could not have made, Kennedy had said. It sobered their faces as they warmed themselves around the refurbished fire.

"We've got to go down there," Lambert was saying. "There's nothing to go back for."

"What about Kennedy and Marstom? Do you think they can travel?" Fox showed his weariness now, but his voice was firm. "We could hold up here another day, if necessary. There's protection here, and fuel."

"The sleep did them good," Lambert said. "They need food, and medicine, as well as rest, and they won't find those things here."

"You think we'll find them—" he jerked his thumb over his shoulder—"down there?"

"We won't know until we try it."

So it was decided. Marstom's cough was noticeably better, and Lars no longer felt the feverish heat in his cheeks; his eyes felt sore, and his bones ached, but he decided that mostly he felt hungry, and dirty, and tired.

They moved down the valley. Jerry Klein was himself again, a little shame-faced as he picked the lead down the rocky slope and stopped to help the sick men. There was a faint trail through the scrub trees, and after two or three hours of trudging downward, they found the forest gave way to a grassy meadow.

Above and below them the fog grew thinner, breaking in patches to let the orange light down. More and more frequently Fox signaled a stop as he studied the gray mists below with field glasses. There was no sound but the scrape of their boots, yet the air seemed charged with tension as they moved on. And then they saw Jerry Klein stop, wave his hand violently and peer down the slope.

They froze in their tracks. The fog below had broken, momentarily, and something had appeared, far below them, for the barest instant. At least they *thought* they saw something.

"Did you see it?" Lambert asked Lars.

"Something—I couldn't tell what."

"We'll stop here," Fox said. "Stay down. That fog bank is breaking. There's *something* down there."

Even as he spoke, Lars felt a breeze pass down the valley, ruffling the grass, and quite suddenly the fog was gone, sunlight streamed down, and they saw the whole valley revealed before them.

They stared unbelieving, wordless.

When Lars described it later, he knew exactly the impression he got that first strange moment when the fog passed. It was as though they had been standing in a darkened theater, and suddenly the curtain had been raised to reveal an incredible stage, a fantastic wonderland. But now he stood rooted like the rest, not thinking, hardly able to comprehend the thing in the valley below them.

It was a city—there was no doubt of that. Towers and spires rose one above the other, wildly, higgledy-piggledy, in utter defiance of gravity. The place was a blaze of flickering color, a confusing, shifting, changing assembly of buildings, arches, spires, bridges—tier upon tier of buildings rising with no semblance of order or harmony, a colorful, incredible riot of architecture.

And as they watched it, *it changed*.

A glistening tower of blue shifted to glowing pink, became misty, spread and sank, and in its place was a needle-pointed spire. Suddenly a great curving bridgeway sprung up from one side, moved swiftly in a graceful arch to the top of the spire. There was constant movement, constant change. Lars rubbed his eyes, and heard Commander Fox's hoarse voice saying, "It can't be. *It can't possibly be.*"

Lars knew what he meant. The colors, the spires, the shifting buildings, the tiny moving figures they could see on the bridges and causeways were only a part of the unbelievable scene before them. A city, yes; even a strange city they could have believed, but this city in the valley was beyond credibility.

Because the entire city, with no visible support of any kind, was floating gently two hundred feet off the ground.

* * *

Once when Lars had been very small, he had seen a traveling magician draw yard upon yard of brightly colored silk from a tiny vase the size of a thimble in his hand. He remembered the day very clearly, and he remembered how frightened he had been, for his reason had told him that that much silk could not possibly come from so small a space, yet his eyes insisted that it had. Years later he understood that both his eyes and his reason had been right. The silks had only *appeared* to come from the tiny vase, but understanding had never restored his broken faith in traveling magicians.

That was the feeling he had now as he stared at the incredible city floating high above the valley floor. It couldn't be true, yet he was seeing it. It was there before his eyes. When he closed his eyes and reopened them, it was still there.

He saw now why Kennedy had been so confused. He understood why Kennedy had said that nothing human could have built that city.

"So these are your aliens," Lambert said as Fox pulled the field glasses from his eyes. "The messages from the *Planetfall* were right. They did contact an alien race here."

Fox said nothing. His eyes were very bright as he stared at the city in the valley.

"But whatever they contacted destroyed their ship," Lambert continued.

"We don't know that!" Fox snapped. "We haven't found it but we don't know these—creatures—are hostile." He looked from man to man. "We have to know that. That means we have to go down there. But not all at once. I'll go down alone, while the rest of you keep under cover."

"I'll go with you," said Lambert.

"Suppose they simply destroy anything that comes near?" Tom Lorry cautioned.

"That's a chance we'll have to take. Keep covered." Fox nodded to Lambert. "Let's go."

Slowly, Fox and Lambert started down the slope. The sun was high, burning away the last vestiges of fog. Lars sat stone-like, gripping his knees as the two men disappeared behind a knoll of rock, reappeared farther, moving toward the city.

Then, suddenly they stopped, appeared to be conferring; they took a few more steps, and stopped again.

Something was wrong. Their steps seemed to be labored, as though they were wading through knee-deep mud.

"Can you see anything?" Marstom whispered.

Lars shook his head. "Something's holding them back. They're trying to hail the city."

"They're fools! They could be wiped out like—"

"But nothing's wiping them out. They just aren't moving ahead any more."

The men had turned back, moving more easily. They turned again down the valley, starting at a run, and again their footsteps slowed. Through the glasses Lars saw Fox bend down, examine the ground minutely. Then the Commander moved forward alone, struggling to drag his feet, until he came to a complete halt, panting. He stood stock-still, facing the city for a long moment; then he turned back, rejoined Lambert, and they trudged back up the slope to the party.

They were still panting when they reached the waiting group. "Can't do it," Fox said. "There's some sort of energy field; it's like slogging through waist-deep mud."

"Could you see anything?" Lorry asked.

"No sign that they've spotted us."

"Maybe I should try," said Lorry.

"Listen," Lambert said quietly.

There was silence as they blinked at him.

"Didn't you hear it?"

"I—I heard *something,"* said Lars suddenly. "Not a sound, but something—almost in my head."

"Yes, yes!" Lambert nodded. "I heard it down there, clearly—something I couldn't understand."

"'Let the boy come forth,'" Walter Fox said slowly.

"That was it! I'm sure of it."

"I heard it too," said Fox. "I can hear it now. 'Let the boy come forth.'"

"What boy?" Lorry asked. Then his eyes rested on Lars.

Lars felt it now, deep within him, a frightening sensation, as if something were calling him, drawing him. "They want me," he said. "I don't know how they're doing it, but they want me."

"This is impossible," Fox snapped. "There's no sound."

"I'd better go," Lars said. "Somebody's got to contact them. If they want me, I'll go."

He shifted his pack from his shoulders, straightened up to his full height. He was frightened, but the thing in his mind that was calling him was not threatening. It was urgent, and powerful, and yet curiously gentle. He didn't even look at the men. He started down the path.

"Lars!" Walter Fox ran after him, gripped his arm. "Do you know what you're doing, son?"

Lars blinked down at the Commander's weary face. Fox's voice was hoarse, his gray eyes pleading. It seemed to Lars that he had never really seen Walter Fox before. The iron-and-steel facade had melted away, and a small and humble man stood there, gripping his arm, begging him to listen.

"I've wanted this all my life," Fox was saying. "I knew we'd find it sometime, I've wanted so badly to find it—"

"Find it?" Lars shook his head in confusion.

"Other life, other creatures than men, intelligent creatures," Fox cried. "Men couldn't be alone in all this endless universe. Can you see that? There had to be other creatures, *good* creatures."

"What are you trying to say?"

"If you find them, down there, don't spoil it for us. If they are good, trust them. Make them know that we are good, too. Offer them friendship. This is not the time for hate or fear or mistrust."

Lars nodded. "I know," he said. "I'll try not to spoil it."

He started down the slope, leaving Fox and the others watching. His eyes were fixed on the city as the towering buildings grew larger. He reached the valley floor, and stopped, as the urging deep in his mind increased. *They were watching him, waiting for him, eagerly.* He stepped out again as a cold edge of fear gnawed at his stomach. He clenched his fists at his side as he moved closer.

At first he thought that the buildings were growing larger, but then he saw that the city was dropping down to meet him. Gently, like a feather, it settled to the ground, and he could see bridges and buildings lined with tiny figures watching him. Ahead was a gate, high and luminous, shimmering as he drew nearer, until he was standing before it.

The gate opened before him, noiselessly, and the "sounds" in his mind seemed to swell, excitedly, as he walked through, like the babble of a thousand voices.

And then, inside, he heard a voice in his ear, a *real* voice so familiar that he whirled with a cry when he heard it, and stopped face to face with Peter Brigham.

11

THE ALIEN LAND

FOR LARS the shock of seeing Peter was almost overwhelming.

Lars was hungry, and dirty, and bone-weary; he could still feel the hot afterglow of his fever; his feet were sore, and it had seemed as he approached the city that every step was the last he could force his aching legs to carry him. But it was more than that. Too much had happened too fast. Too much that had happened was utterly unbelievable, and yet demanded belief because his eyes and senses said it was so. Since the group had started up the mountain days before, it had been like a nightmare that would not end, full of impossible occurrences and half-suggested horrors.

And now, like an island appearing in a sea of chaos, Peter. Lars didn't know whether to laugh or cry. It was Peter, beyond doubt. The gates had fallen open, and he had walked into a high-roofed, brilliantly lighted entranceway, with the strange city shifting and glowing before his eyes through a nearby archway, and there was Peter, very much alive, very much here on Wolf IV, utterly unexplainable.

Lars had cried out in pure relief to see a familiar face, but now a flood of memories swept through his mind, confused, jumbled, only half-real, but memories just the same. The despair he had felt when the deserters had bolted camp, marooning the rest of them on this alien land; the bitter struggle up the mountainside to the wreck they had been sure was the *Planetfall*, and the almost unspeakable disappointment that had met them when they reached it—he remembered.

Peter had deserted them. He had run out on them with Salter and Leeds and the rest.

"What are you doing here?" Lars blurted. "What did you do with the ship? The others, where are they?" He stared at Peter, his eyes blazing.

"Never mind, it doesn't matter right now," Peter said quickly. He glanced behind him at the great entranceway. "You've got to—"

"Doesn't matter! We'd be dead by now if it wasn't for Fox, after you and your pals ran out on us. What do you mean, it doesn't matter?"

"We may *all* be dead if you don't listen," Peter snapped. "Or as good as dead." There was urgency in Peter's voice, wide open warning in his eyes. "I know what you think, but I didn't run out on you. There isn't time to explain it now. Later, if we're lucky. They'll be here any minute, so listen. Close your mind to everything you can. Make it a blank, don't think of *anything* if you can help it when they come, or they'll be picking your brain like a walnut. But don't be surprised at anything, and don't do anything to alarm them."

Lars nodded once and fell silent. He didn't understand what Peter was saying, but he heard the urgency and dread in his voice. Whatever had happened before could be settled in good time; there was an immediate menace here, overriding everything else.

His eyes took in all the detail of the huge entranceway. The walls were smooth, curving up into a high, vaulted ceiling. There was a light which seemed to emanate from the walls themselves, softly pink, shimmering. Through the archway he could see the buildings, piled in a fantastic jumble about each other. At first there had been no sign of life; now there was a growing buzz of excitement which seemed to come from all sides of him, though he could hear nothing. It was as though he was *feeling* the hum and excitement of the city deep in his mind.

And then there was a lull, as though thousands of people had suddenly taken a deep breath. The archway was breaking open, *dissolving* in brilliantly glowing particles as three figures moved down a ramp and came toward them. Lars had not seen them approach; suddenly they were there, as if they materialized out of thin air. They reached Peter and Lars in a moment, staring at Lars with unabashed curiosity as they came nearer.

They looked like human beings. They were tall and slender, two men and a woman, moving with an easy grace that seemed very odd, until Lars noticed that their feet were hardly touching the ground. The woman creature had light hair; the men were dark, their faces guarded.

They showed no hostility, but their actions were as strange as their uncanny similarity to Earthmen in appearance. They reached out to touch Lars' clothes, to peer into his eyes questioningly, to rub a finger across his unshaven chin. Occasionally they paused in their inspection to look at one another and nod, then resumed their examination.

Exactly like children examining a new toy, a toy they are a little afraid of, Lars thought. He glanced at Peter, but Peter shook his head almost imperceptibly.

Finally Lars could stand the silent inspection no longer. "I'm an Earthman," he said in a voice that was too loud for the silence. "My name is Heldrigsson. I'm one of the crew of a Star Ship that came from a planet called—"

He broke off sharply. The three City-people were paying no attention to his words. Peter shook his head again. "It won't do any good to talk to them. They have no spoken language."

"But how do they—" Lars groped for the right word—*"talk?"*

"They've got a lot slicker means of communicating than we have," said Peter heavily. "How did you know they wanted you to come down here? It was you they wanted, you know, none of the rest. But how did you know that?"

Lars had no answer that made any sense. *I just knew it,* he thought. *My ears didn't hear anything, but I heard just the same.* How could he describe the eerie—*feeling*—that had struck him out there in the valley? As he tried to think of the right words, he felt the same feeling stirring again in his mind. Weary as he was, he felt himself growing tense. There was an abrupt, ridiculous mental picture of someone gently but firmly prying the lid off a coffee can, and then, suddenly, he knew they were in his mind, probing with soft, feathery fingers. He *felt* their questions, although there was no sound, and they seemed to pick up his answers from his mind before they reached his tongue.

No wonder they don't talk! he thought wildly. *They don't need to talk!*

The woman looked at him in surprise. *Talk? what is 'talk'?* It came clearly, a direct question. All three City-people were looking at him in puzzlement.

Talk. Making sounds that mean what you are thinking—

They snatched the answer before it came from his lips, and they looked at each other, still puzzled, and then laughed. They didn't really understand what he meant at all.

The woman pointed a finger at him. *Who are you?*

An Earthman. I'm called Heldrigsson. Lars Heldrigsson.

Again the puzzlement and confusion. *Earthman? Heldrigsson? Lars? Many thoughts in your mind, all mean you—*

I'm like him. Lars pointed to Peter.

They understood that, and it seemed to fill them with sudden eagerness and excitement. The men's impassive faces broke into smiles as they nodded to each other, and Lars caught the stream of thought as it passed between them: *—we were right, the two are indeed the same, then! It is good, good! Just as the Masters promised, sometime—*

Lars blinked. "The Masters" had not been a word, but a thought, a mental picture of greatness and inaccessibility and reverence. It was almost as though the City-people had hushed their thought-voices as they mentioned the name, and bowed their heads gently. *Yes, it is just as the Masters promised.*

And then the woman was looking at him sharply. Like the others, she was dressed in a formless gray cloak of feathery soft material, and her hair seemed to shimmer in the light from the walls. She was very beautiful, her face childlike and yet gentle, her eyes gray and wide spaced. *Then you come like all the others, from—* She seemed to grapple for a picture that was beyond her capabilities.

From another star, Lars thought. From a planet called Earth, third from the sun—

Sun?

Our star. We call it Sol. Far away—

Away? What is that?

From another land, not this world at all.

But you must be weary, coming so far.

Lars stared. She was picturing him walking. *We came in a Star Ship, the* Ganymede.

Confusion again. *Why did you do that?*

To find another Star Ship that was lost here.

But why do you use these—Star Ships?

Now it was Lars' turn to be puzzled. He turned to Peter. "I think I'm missing something somehow."

Peter nodded. "I've been on the same treadmill for days. They just can't conceive of any other world but this planet. They don't know what you mean about 'another world' and 'across space' and things like that. They can't seem to grasp what a Star Ship is used for, or why anyone would need to use one."

Once again Lars tried to convey the idea of crossing depths of space enclosed and propelled and protected by a shell of metal and plastic, but it was useless. He was so weary he could hardly keep his own thoughts straight, and this incredible means of conversation was quickly wearing away his last vestige of control. "Look, can't they get me something to eat, or let me wash up and get some sleep or something?" he burst out to Peter.

"Go ahead and ask them," said Peter. "Give them a good sharp mental picture of what you want, and how lousy you feel, and what you'd like right now."

Lars tried it. He conjured up an image of weariness and hunger that would have torn the heart out of a statue, and visualized a steaming hot shower and a clean warm bed. To his amazement the three City-people caught the images perfectly. A rush of sympathy and apology poured from their minds. *We are tiring you and you need rest. Come, we will make you comfortable. Later we will—talk.*

"But what about the others?" Lars said loud. "They have no food. Kennedy and Marstom are sick. And there are two more down on the other side of the mountain."

"They're here," Peter said quickly. "The others will be brought in, don't worry. Just come along now."

Lars needed no further urging. He followed the strange people into the city.

It was not until then that Lars got a good look at the city. Tired as he was, he watched the jumbled panorama spread before him with eyes wide with amazement. It was like a city built with brightly colored children's blocks of every imaginable size and shape. There were gaudy arches and glistening spires. Sweeping walkways moved between the buildings that hung individually in the air, some high, some low, some large and square, some low and discoid, some round and transparent as bubbles, spinning slowly through the air. There seemed to be no planning of the city; it hung there willy-nilly, yet in its very disorganization there was a wild incredible sort of beauty. Nothing here was ugly. There was no dirt, no grayness. The City-people were everywhere, thronging the walkways and arches, moving up over the sweeping curves of bridges, and everywhere the buzz of activity and life washed over Lars like a wave. There were ancient City-people with long beards and white hair; many were young with the same peculiar young-old appearance that the woman who was leading them had shown. An occasional woman passed with a pink baby in her arms, and a string of youngsters fell in behind them, watching with great curiosity as they moved through the city.

Their method of travel was also confusing. They started

off walking, or so it seemed to Lars, yet they seemed to move great distances with very little effort, and in very little time. One instant they were moving up on an arching bridge; the next moment the bridge was behind them. Lars shook his head sharply and looked at Peter in confusion.

"You'll get used to it," Peter said. "They're only 'walking' in deference to us."

"How do they usually get around?"

"I'm not sure what you'd call it. You know the tricks some of the teleps back home use—putting a ball in a box, and then making it pop through without opening the box? It seems to be pretty much the same. They want to go somewhere, and *zip* there they are! They took me out that way once, and I was sick all over everything. Since then they've slowed down to a fast run for me."

They had been moving toward a long, low building of pale blue color, floating high above the majority of the buildings. This one had a crystal spire that rose a hundred feet in the air and sparkled like an icicle in the sunlight. Now, even as Lars watched, they were suddenly inside the building in a long sloping corridor. It seemed to be a library or lounge. Along one side curving sheets of plastic material stood near the wall, with a bank of control buttons at the side. A closer look revealed them to be viewing plates, for one of them was glowing a dull blue, but there was no image, that Lars could see, on the screen. Quite abruptly the blue screen flickered and blinked out, becoming dull gray like the rest.

"Our 'study'," Peter said softly. "We have living quarters at the end there."

They approached the end of the corridor, where a tall thin door-like slab lay against the pale green wall. Its fluted edges were visible, clinging to the wall, and there was no knob. The three City-people stopped, looking around at

Lars. Once again he felt the feathery flutter of their thought-fingers in his mind. *For you. Your quarters. You will find food and sleeping clothes inside.*

He nodded, and waited for them to open the door, but nothing happened. The three were watching him closely. "They want you to open the door," Peter whispered.

"But there's no knob."

They only waited a moment as Lars stared helplessly at the door. Then he felt, rather than heard a tiny sigh from the City-people. The woman touched the door with her finger, and it dissolved into mist, then vanished, revealing a large comfortable room beyond. He stepped in, still feeling the wave of disappointment in the City-peoples' minds, and the fragments of thought: *He is like the other. But perhaps with lessons he too—*

And then Lars and Peter were in the room, and the door had reappeared, leaving them alone. To one side was a bath, with hot water running and sending up heart-warming clouds of steam; there were two beds, soft and inviting, though they were really only pallets floating three feet off the ground; and near the beds two trays of food that made Lars' mouth water.

They were in their quarters. Prisoners? It would seem so, and yet the three City-people had no hostility in their minds. On the contrary, there had been a haunting aura of deference as they had probed his mind, as though he were not a prisoner so much as an honored and somehow very important guest. There had been a sense of eagerness as they had examined him, of watchfulness and hopefulness.

And that strong last impression, rising again to Lars' mind: *Perhaps with lessons—*

He saw the hot water, the beds, the food, but there was something even more important first. He turned to Peter. This city and the people here were like a fantastic dream, but Peter was no dream. Peter Brigham was Peter Brigham, human flesh and blood. A rested, warm, well-fed Peter Brigham who, for all his urgent warning, did not seem too much afraid of these City-people. Indeed, he seemed to accept them very calmly. If there was something hazy and unreal about these aliens of Wolf IV, there was nothing hazy about Peter, nor about the things that Lars knew were true:

That there had been a Star Ship named *Ganymede* which had brought them there, him and Peter and twenty other Earthmen.

That Peter had joined the deserters to seize the ship, and had somehow managed to spirit it from its landing-site.

That a Star Ship the size of the *Ganymede* does not just vanish into thin air, on Wolf IV or any other place.

That sometime, many months before, another Star Ship named *Planetfall* had made a landing on this planet, and had also vanished.

Lars turned to Peter. "'All right. The food will wait. I want some answers, and I want them right now."

"They'll make more sense when you're rested up." Peter said.

"I think they'd better make sense right now," Lars said. "Where are those ships? Where are the men?"

With a sigh, Peter walked across the room. As he approached the far wall, it began to fade away, just as the door had, revealing a wide panorama of the city below them. "Come here," said Peter. "I can answer one of your questions without any trouble at all."

Lars approached the window. The bright lights of the city caught his eyes like a display of fireworks.

"You're right," Peter said slowly. "The *Ganymede* didn't vanish into space and nobody lifted it off the planet, either." He pointed. "Down there, on the ramps."

It was a more substantial structure than the others in the city, heavy and solid, forming two long narrow cradles. And in the cradles were two long Star Ships, almost twins, lying side by side.

Lars would have recognized the *Ganymede* anywhere. He had never seen the other ship before, but he knew without question that it was the *Star Ship Planetfall*.

This, then, had been the end of her journey.

12

WHO ARE THEY?

PETER was gone when Lars finally awoke. He did not know how long he had slept. When he had crawled into the bed he had been too weary even to check his chronometer. The hot bath had been wonderful; there were no robot scrubbers like you found in Earth shower stalls, and the water had come from all sides like a fountain, but he got clean and warm, and found some of the feathery gray clothing ready for him when he finished. He had eaten like a starved man, and was asleep two minutes after he closed his eyes.

Now he looked about the room, concern shocking him into wakefulness. There was no sign of Peter, but the table was again sct with food. It didn't look like any food he had ever seen, but the piquant texture and taste removed any lingering suspicions of its quality. Nothing could taste so good, and not be nourishing. There was a plate of meaty-tasting stuff, some spicy soup, and what he took to be vegetables, in spite of their pale blue color. The plates refilled automatically as he ate, although no one entered the room; when he was finally filled, the food, table and all, vanished, leaving only a faint pleasant odor in the air.

This off-again-on-again business was startling, to say the least; Lars felt a little queasy as he walked about the room, inspecting the smooth material of the walls, watching the large window grow transparent as he moved near it. The two ships still lay in their racks below, as though they had been there for years, but the sight of them perked Lars back to the thousand unanswered questions in his mind.

He felt a wave of relief as he heard Peter's voice, saw him walking in through the door, which had become thin and gauzy, barely concealing the study room beyond. "About time you were stirring," Peter was saying.

"Where have you been?"

"Having my lessons."

"What lessons?"

"You'll see, I think." Peter glanced through the window. "Oh, they're still here," he said, nodding to the ships. "They're not going anywhere."

"But where are the crews?" A horrible thought struck Lars. "These people haven't *assimilated* them somehow, have they? I mean, dug around in their minds until they were picked clean, and then—"

"No, no, nothing like that," said Peter. "The crew of the *Planetfall* is in the same place as the crew of the *Ganymede,* with the sole exceptions of you and me." There was a note of resignation and hopelessness in Peter's voice.

"Where is that?"

"In a special vault they've built for them in the depths of the city."

"You mean they've killed them?"

"Oh, no, they're not dead. They're asleep. They've been fed and cared for ever so carefully, but they're kept sleeping, and as far as I can determine, these City-people have no intention in the world of waking them up, ever. That's why I warned you to go easy until we saw how they received you, because I've got a hunch that if they decide to put us to sleep, nobody is ever going to wake us up."

"Wait a minute," Lars said, confused. "I left Fox and Lambert and the others up on the hillside. They couldn't even get close to this place."

"They're here now. I doubt if they ever got a look at the inside of the city. I think they were put to sleep before the City-people brought them in. But I don't know any way to tell that for sure."

Lars stared at Peter, then walked over to the window again. "You still haven't told me how you got here, or how the ship got here, for that matter."

Peter shrugged. "They brought us here. Don't ask me how, because I can't tell you."

"But you bolted that night with Salter and Leeds!" Lars accused.

"Not because I wanted to, believe me. I never dreamed that Salter would try to make a break for it so soon."

"Then it *was* planned in advance."

"Of course it was planned in advance," Peter said irritably. "You people went around that ship after the showdown with Fox acting as though you thought if you didn't look at it, maybe it would just go away. Salter and his pals were planning a break with the ship from the minute the mutiny fell through. They didn't cut me in on it until we were actually organizing the landing party, and then they only told me to be on my toes when the time came. They had no intention of running into any aliens on Wolf IV.

They thought that the landing parties would leave the ship under a light guard, and that they could break away and seize it, and then head out. Which was what they did, up to a point."

"And when they got back to Earth?"

"No problem. Who'd be there to argue any story they told? The Colonial Service would have to believe them."

"So they planned to murder or maroon anyone that didn't go along with them," said Lars bitterly.

"Now you're getting the picture," said Peter. "I got just an inkling of it. Salter was still sore that I didn't vote with him before, and I hoped I could spot the trouble and tip off the rest of you when the time came. Trouble was, it came too soon. Salter moved as soon as the rest of you were asleep, and I had the choice of going along quietly or taking a bullet in the head. I chose the former. I thought even at that I might be able to break away and warn the men on the ship."

"So that was how it was," Lars said slowly. Suddenly, he felt as if a great weight had been lifted from his shoulders. He had not realized how much Peter's desertion had hurt, not because of treachery to the ship and its crew, but very personally. He couldn't believe that Peter had done what he had done willfully. "I'm glad it was that way," he said. "I'm really glad."

"You thought something else, maybe?"

"I—didn't know what to think."

"I suppose it must have looked pretty mean. Oh, I know I've acted like a fool about some things on this trip, but I wasn't ready to join this scheme, believe me. I felt pretty dirty helping Salter and Leeds get those boats across the river, and then cutting them loose. And of course, when we got back to where the *Ganymede* had landed, it was gone, and I didn't have a chance to sound an alarm after all."

"Gone!" said Lars. "You mean you didn't move it at all?"

"It wasn't there to be moved. You should have seen Jeff Salter's face! It would have made you feel lots better about that trip over the mountain. He'd figured it was all smooth as oiled silk from then on out, and then whammo, no ship. We were in as bad shape as the ones we'd run out on. Only Salter wasn't exactly the leader type. It scared him silly when we came down and found that ship gone. He was all over the place, sending us out to scour the area, he thought we might have missed the way, but scared to wait by himself for fear something would jump on him from the woods."

"But what did happen?" asked Lars.

"We went over to the place where the ship had been, and began looking around for it, and then, just like that, we weren't *there,* any more, but *here.* In the city. In a room with a dozen aliens, stripped of our weapons. I still haven't found out what they did with our machine pistols. And every single one of the men dead asleep except me."

"Except you," Lars repeated.

"That's right."

"First you, then me. What's so special about *us?*"

"You find me the answer for that, and we'd be on our way out of here," Peter said grimly. "I don't know why, and the City-people here either can't or won't tell me why."

"Coincidence?" said Lars.

Peter snorted. "Do you think so?"

"But what else? What have they been doing with you?"

"Giving me lessons."

"Look, lessons mean teaching something," Lars protested. "What are they trying to teach you?"

"I've been trying to find that out ever since they started.

I haven't an inkling. But I know one thing. From the minute I turned up in this city, the City-people have been trying to teach me *something,* with every technique and resource at their disposal." Peter gave him a grin. "So chew on that for a while."

"Can you show me around this place, or are we locked in?"

"We're free as the wind except at lesson time," said Peter wryly.

"Then show me around a bit."

They left the quarters and started out on a tour of the remarkable city, Peter with a firm step, Lars walking in fear and trembling lest the airy structure of the place should suddenly tumble down upon them like a house of cards. They walked across a high bridge from their building (which Lars could have sworn was not there when they had first come) and around a long circular staircase down toward the ground. The end of the staircase was twenty feet up, so that it appeared that they must turn around and come back, but as they neared the end, the building, staircase and all, obligingly drifted down to firm ground for them.

Lars shook his head uneasily. "This is what I can't understand," he said, pointing to the staircase, which was rising up again. "This business of now-it's-one-place-now-another. I see it happening, but I can't quite get myself to believe it. Things don't just up and vanish."

"It's the way they live," Peter said. "Your bed last night, was it comfortable?"

"Perfectly."

"Good and steady? It didn't lurch around when you crawled in?"

"No, it was steady enough."

"Well, have you figured out what held it up, yet?"

"No."

"I don't think you're going to, either, because *nothing* was holding it up. These City-people have almost complete telepathic control of everything around them. Just the way the telep on 3-V back home can control the ball in the box."

"Then these things are a result of extra-sensory perception?" Lars asked incredulously. "That's impossible! Nobody has ever learned how to control extra-sensory powers like this, not even the most skillful telep on Earth."

"The City-people do," said Peter. "It's what we think of as extra-sensory power, but with them it's refined beyond anything we've ever seen on Earth. With these people it's completely unconscious: telepathy, telekinesis, teleportation, anything you want to call it. They control it. Their whole culture and civilization is based on it."

Lars shook his head in confusion. "Our scientists on Earth have been working with ESP for centuries and they've never learned how to control it," he said. "Some of them even claim it never *can* be controlled or useful for anything."

"Well, these people can certainly use it," Peter said. "You notice what a hodge-podge this city is?"

Lars nodded. "It looks as though the city planners were out to lunch when the plans were drawn up."

"There weren't any city planners. These people arrange things strictly to suit themselves. They can move a single molecule or the side of a mountain, individually or collectively, just by deciding that they want it moved. Their houses float when they want them to, or sit on the ground when they want them to. If they get bored with one kind of house they rearrange it into another kind. Since they travel around almost entirely by teleportation, the doors and windows are ninety per cent decoration. That's why you see doorways like that." Peter pointed to an oval-shaped building they were passing. It had pale orange doorways shaped like tall slender triangles.

"But what do they live on?" Lars asked. "They do eat, don't they? How do they grow crops on a barren place like this?"

"That's just it, they don't need to grow crops! There's plenty of plant and animal life on the planet, with plenty of protein, and fat, and carbohydrate molecules on hand. They simply rearrange them into palatable combinations when they get hungry. I suppose they could start with subatomic particles and work themselves up a genuine Montana beef steak, if they knew what one was."

"By ESP," said Lars.

"By ESP." Peter grinned. "There's nothing magical or fantastic about it. You've seen enough of our own teleps to know extra-sensory powers exist. These people just know how to control those powers."

They moved on through the maze of buildings. "Can you show me the ships?" Lars wanted to know.

"Afraid not. They're forbidden. The City-people don't want us near them."

"How about the place where the men are—sleeping?"

"That's even worse. The City-people themselves don't like to go there. You might talk them into taking you there later, but right now I don't think we should do anything to ruffle our hosts."

"I suppose not." Lars shook his head. "The thing that bothers me the most about this whole thing is how much these City-people look like humans. They've got *fingerprints*, did you notice? And their skin, and their hair, their musculature—I couldn't tell the difference, unless I looked at their faces, and *then* I couldn't be sure."

"I know exactly what you mean," Peter said grimly.

"The resemblance is more striking every time you see them close up. In fact, for my money, the resemblance is too striking."

"What do you mean?"

"I mean that I'd swear by everything I believe in that these people are Earthmen." Peter made an angry gesture. "It's just about driving me crazy. They *look* like Earthmen, but they don't begin to act like them. They're like children. Their whole life revolves on this extra-sensory control of things. They use ESP just as naturally as they breathe, and yet they have no sense of logic whatever. Their minds are totally alien. They have no concept of science, or of machinery, or anything else. They don't know about anything outside this city and this planet, and they don't care, or didn't until now. I'm certain that they honestly don't know what we *mean* when we tell them we come from another planet of another star. But who are they? Where do they come from?"

"Have you asked them?" Lars said.

"I've asked them until I was black in the face. I might as well not have bothered. They didn't even understand the question."

They moved about the city until the sky began to darken, and then turned back to their quarters. As they walked through the corridor with the viewscreens, Lars stopped short. "Hold it," he said. "I thought you told me they had no concept of science or mechanics. How did they get those things?"

"That's a good question," Peter said. "Try one once, and see what you think."

Lars sat down before one of the gray screens. "How do you work it?"

Peter opened a wall slot and withdrew a small, flat cartridge. He fit this onto a spool at the side of the screen.

Abruptly the screen leaped into life with the pale blue color Lars had seen before. There was a flickering geometric pattern, but no image that Lars could recognize. "Now what?"

"It's a little tricky," Peter conceded. "That's not a 3-V screen, and the tape on that cartridge doesn't work quite like a 3-V tape. You've got to—well, sort of tune in on it yourself. Watch it for a minute."

Lars watched the screen. At first there was nothing. Then gradually, he noticed a tingling in his fingers and toes. Images began to form on the screen, or in his mind, he couldn't tell which for sure. Not a story, just a series of impressions drifting through his mind as he stared. He felt his scalp crawl. "Say, what is this thing doing?" he said, jumping up from it angrily.

The images on the screen blinked out.

"It's projecting," said Peter. "Our 3-Vs depend on visual images and audible sounds to get through to us. This little gadget by-passes the eyes and ears and goes right straight in. It projects mental images instead of visual images. That's what you were picking up. The thing can be reversed so that *you* project to *it* and it records like a tape recorder."

"But what was I seeing?"

Peter shrugged. "To the City-people what you just saw was a history text."

"It didn't look like a history text to me. It didn't make any sense at all."

"Well, it's the closest to recorded history that they have. Oh, they have a word-of-mouth sort of history. Maybe I should say 'word-of-mind.' You know, legends and superstitions. But as for recording history—" Peter scowled at the viewscreen. "I'm dead sure these people never made these screens. They couldn't have. They couldn't know how. They don't know enough about science in general, or electronics in particular, to have done it."

They walked through the filmy door into their quarters. "But who did make the screens, then?" asked Lars.

"I don't know," said Peter. "But I've got an idea. Maybe I'm crazy, but I'd swear that there is another kind of creature on Wolf IV. A creature completely different from these City-people. I don't know where, but I'm sure of it. The City-people know about them, and have been in contact with them, somehow."

Lars chewed his lip. "Wait a minute, you mean the ones they call the Masters?"

"That's right. I get the impression that these other creatures, these Masters, used to be right here among the City-people. These people keep referring to them as 'the Masters that fed us and taught us.' I think the Masters built these viewscreens."

"But where are they now?"

"I don't know," said Peter, "and I don't seem to find out. The City-people aren't *afraid* of them, exactly. They seem to be in awe of them. The 'Masters' keep coming up whenever you talk to the City-people, but you can't pin them down to just what they are, or where they are."

"But there must be *something* we can get hold of," Lars said in exasperation.

Peter was silent for a moment. Then he said, "What did you find up on the mountain ridge? What was the wreck that we saw in Kennedy's pictures?"

Lars told him. Peter stared. "The *Argonaut!* You mean the Earth ship that took the Long Passage?"

"That's right."

"But it's been lost for centuries."

"It isn't lost any more. It crashed up there."

"That's very strange," said Peter, "because one of the

few things I *am* sure of about these people is that they know about that wreck up there, and they're afraid of it."

"*Afraid* of it?"

"They never go there. "It's a 'forbidden place.' They can't say why, or won't. They don't even want to talk about it. Which is particularly odd when you consider that they haven't the least fear or interest in the two ships here in the city. They don't want *us* to go near them, but they aren't afraid of them."

"Anything else that you're sure about?" Lars asked. "I mean, we might as well cover the board while we're at it."

"Just one thing," said Peter. "The City-people are desperately afraid of the crewmen of both ships!"

"But I thought you said they were asleep."

"They are, but the people are still afraid of them. They take care of them as if they were fusion bombs approaching critical. The thought of wakening them literally scares the City-people out of their wits."

Lars thought that over. "But they aren't afraid of us!" he protested. "I mean you and me. Or at least, if they are, they hide it pretty well. This gets crazier and crazier every minute, and we always seem to slam up against the same brick wall: exactly what is so special about *you and me?*"

But they had no answer to that question. Food had appeared as they were talking, and they settled down glumly to eat. "They'll be coming to give you your first lesson when we're finished," Peter said. "Maybe you'll have some brilliant ideas along the way. I sure haven't had any."

"But there's *nothing*—" Lars protested.

"There *has* to be something that's important to them that we just can't see," said Peter. "But what it could be is beyond me. I hate to admit that I'm whipped, but I've got no choice on this one."

"There's only one thing," Lars said.

Peter stopped with his food halfway to his mouth. "What?"

"Oh, nothing," Lars muttered in disgust. "We're different from the rest of the crew in one way, but I don't see how it could make much difference."

"What are you talking about?"

"Our ages," said Lars. "It's the only imaginable thing that could distinguish us from the rest of the crewmen in the eyes of these strangers, that could make us any different from Commander Fox, or Lambert, or Salter, or any of the others."

"You mean—"

"Yes," said Lars. *"Both of us are young."*

13

THE PLACE OF THE MASTERS

IT WAS so obvious, and yet so ridiculous, that they both burst into gales of laughter. It had been there staring them in the face from the first, yet it made no sense at all.

"But it's true," Lars said flushing. "We're both just eighteen. The next youngest man on the crew is Mangano, and he's twenty-six."

"Maybe they figure we'll be the tenderest for roasting," said Peter.

"Well, why not?"

"It doesn't add up to anything, that's why," said Peter.

"Neither does anything else around this place to us. But obviously it adds up to the City-people, or they wouldn't make a distinction like this. What other difference can you suggest?" Lars rose from the meal and walked over to the window, stared out across the city. The sky was dark now, but the bright lights of the buildings made it seem like daylight outside. "The way I see it, we've been tripping over everything in sight, and losing track of the one thing that we've just got to remember: that there are answers to this whole business. There *must* be answers, simple answers. We can't see how, but somehow the pieces must fit together."

"I wonder," said Peter sourly.

"Look, we'll think of something. Can you brief me on these lessons a little bit?"

"Why not ask your tutors?" Peter said. "Here they are now."

The woman and one of the men who had met Lars at the gate had suddenly appeared at the door to their quarters. It was the first Lars had seen of them since he had arrived, but now he felt a much different kind of apprehension than he had then. *At least,* he thought, *I'm rested and fresh now. They won't catch me off guard.*

They picked it up, and glanced gravely at each other. The woman shook her head. *We are glad you are rested but you must not fight us. There is much you must learn.*

What must I learn? Lars shot at them.

We must teach you what the Masters taught us, of course. She shook her head again, cutting off the question rising to his lips. *Come. We will work out here.*

It was the strangest kind of lesson Lars had ever had in his life. They placed him before one of the gray viewscreens, but they did not activate it at first. Almost at once he felt their probing thought-fingers in his mind. *First you must understand that there is no harm, no pain. We will not hurt you.* It was the woman, who seemed to have taken charge, with the man merely observing.

Lars felt his muscles grow tense. *What are you going to do?*

There is nothing we can do but enter your mind and

guide you. It is you who must do the work. She was gentle, but Lars could sense the unyielding firmness behind the gentleness.

What work? What do you want me to do?

The City-people looked at each other helplessly. Lars caught a drift of thought from the woman: *He doesn't understand. How can we—*

There must be a way, somehow.

When the thoughts were not directed at him, Lars received only a drift; but when they addressed him directly he understood them faultlessly. He realized with a start that he was almost getting used to this silent communication. It was like conversing with a deaf-mute boy he had known years before. The lad could read lips, but could not hear a sound. It had not taken Lars long to learn to speak to him soundlessly, forming his words carefully with his lips only. And now, similarly, he was forming his words in thoughts only.

The City-people had turned to him once again, and this time he felt a shock as they probed deeply, searching the farthest reaches of his mind. He had an eerie feeling, almost like nausea, for a moment; it was like the first downward lurch of an elevator, or the initial shock of free-fall in space, not exactly unpleasant, yet *unsettling*. But now, suddenly he noticed that the viewscreen was glowing faintly! The City-people glanced at each other excitedly, urging him on, but his mind rebelled. He felt himself jerk up like a tightly-reined horse.

No, no! It was the woman, urgent, appealing. *Let yourself go.*

He relaxed for a moment, felt himself breaking free of control again, but this time he was prepared and reined himself in sharply, fighting down the weird sensation.

No, no, please. You must help us, not fight us.

But I don't like it. I can't let myself go. Lars felt the

half-nausea again, and it seemed as though his whole body was drained of strength. *I don't like it.*

But there is no harm.

I still don't like it. Lars felt trapped, helpless against the power of these two minds. *What are you trying to do? What is the purpose of this?*

Amazement from the woman, as though he had suddenly slapped her face. *To teach you, of course. We don't want to frighten you.*

Teach me what?

It was full circle again. The woman and man exchanged grim glances. *The same as with the other one. Blocking, fighting, trying his best to avoid—*

It frightens him. This from the woman. *Can it be that they don't know?*

They must know. They couldn't help but know.

Once again Lars caught the impression of "the Masters" strong in the minds of the City-people. The impression of a very real entity, yet it took no recognizable shape in Lars' mind. He groped, trying to catch the impression, but the woman shook her head. *You are tired. That is enough for* today. *Tomorrow we will try again.*

Wait! Lars jumped to his feet. *There's something I want to know.*

The woman paused, questioningly.

The others. Where are the others who came with me?

A wave of fear, faint but unmistakable. Something became guarded in the woman's eyes. *They are safe. They are sleeping.*

Then wake them up.

Never! Sharp fear flared in her eyes. *No, no, they must remain asleep.*

I don't believe you. I don't think they're here. Lars

watched their faces closely, groped with his mind to catch their response. *I think you've killed them.*

No, no! We could never have done that. The Masters would be angry.

Then take me to them. Show me. Prove that they're still alive.

There was a sound in the door, and Lars saw Peter standing there, watching, his eyes wide. "What are you doing?"

"I told them we want to see the others," Lars snapped. He turned back to the woman. *Take both of us. Both of us want to see.*

The City-people stood transfixed, fear strong in both their minds. Then Lars sensed the shadow of a sigh, a breath of resignation, as the man made a weary gesture with his hands. *All right. We will show you. Come.*

They were afraid. They tried to shield their fear, but Lars could feel it, like an ugly gray blanket, wrapping their thoughts as they led the way down into the vault. They were afraid with an overwhelming, uncontrollable fear. Lars and Peter followed, white-faced, feeling an almost unbearable apprehension themselves as they moved through corridors and down darkened stairways.

"Can you feel it?" Lars whispered as they walked.

"It's about to knock me over," Peter whispered back. "They're practically paralyzed with fear."

"But why should they be? If they have nothing to hide, I mean."

"I don't think that's the thing at all."

Something caught in Lars' mind, and he looked sharply at Peter. "How did you know what I was doing when I asked to come down here? I didn't make a sound."

"I know. I—*felt* it. I couldn't tell what, exactly, but I knew you'd hit them with something."

They finally reached a long, darkened room, far down in the depths of the city. Along both walls of the vault were pallets, floating off the floor. On each pallet was a sleeping man. Lars stared at the figures. Suddenly he felt very cold. They were breathing slowly; some were muttering in their sleep. Occasionally one moved an arm or a leg. Down the right hand side he could see John Lambert, snoring gently. Commander Fox slept beside him. On the far side was Jeff Salter.

You see? All sleeping. All safe. Lars caught the woman's thought, but he also felt the wave of fear emanating from her mind, twisting into his thoughts like an icy finger. Then she turned sharply, almost out of control, and led them upstairs into the cool, pleasant corridor above.

Lars was not sorry to leave the darkened vault. It had been a ghastly sight, but the men were there, alive, sleeping. *Why have you done this?* Lars thought sharply. *Why are you so afraid of them?*

But don't you see? They would destroy us. The Masters warned us.

Who are these Masters?

The woman blinked at him, not comprehending. *The Masters are the Masters. Who else?*

Are they here? In the city?

Oh, no. They left long ago. They have never returned. But when the time is right—

Lars caught the flush of excitement in Peter's eyes. *But the Masters left you orders you have to obey. Is that right?*

Orders? Obey? The Masters knew what was right. Why should we need orders to obey? The woman's confusion was growing. *Surely you understand, it was the Masters who fed us and taught us. We only do as they wish.*

And then Lars saw the question that had to be answered. He looked straight at the woman and put all his power into the query: *What were you before the Masters came?*

For the barest instant Lars felt her fear, the shadow of doubt flitting through her mind, as though he had torn open a door that had long been closed, arousing some timeless, shapeless fear. But then the door closed again, leaving only puzzlement and confusion. *You must go back. You must not come here again.*

Why not? What were you before the Masters came?

Later, he saw what he couldn't just then. "She couldn't answer the question because she didn't understand it," he told Peter, back in their room. "Whatever the Masters were, they obviously blocked out whole chunks of these people's minds."

"But why?" said Peter.

"We may learn that when we learn what the Masters were. But I don't think the City-people are going to tell us. I don't think they know themselves!"

It was Peter who finally broke the deadlock, though in quite a different way than he imagined.

Day had followed day among the City-people of Wolf IV with no appreciable change. Every day both Lars and Peter had two and even three sessions with their tutors, and still they seemed to come no closer to the answers they sought than before. If anything the City-people and their reasons for singling out the two youngest crewmen for attention became more imponderable than ever as the boys saw more of the workings of the city.

They did learn bits and snatches. They learned that death was all but unknown in the city. There were people of all ages there, old and young, but when a death did occur it was a source of city-wide mourning.

Furthermore, Lars was able to confirm his conclusion that he and Peter were allowed to remain awake, of all the crewmen, because of their age. But try as he would he could not discover why their age was considered so important. Even direct questions brought only confused replies. *Why are you keeping us here?* he asked the woman who was working with him, flashing the thought at her without warning. *Why didn't you put us to sleep, too?*

She stared at him for a moment in amazement. Then: *But we could not do that! The Masters would never allow it. You are like us, not like the others.*

Lars had recounted the matter to Peter that evening as they lay in the darkness of their room. "These Masters!" Peter burst out. "Every time we get them in a corner, they bring in the Masters to settle the question as though they were the last possible authority. Have you noticed that? Every time!"

"I know. It's a brick wall. We keep slamming head-on into it. We can't seem to get over it and we can't get under it." Lars stared glumly at the ceiling. "I think they're getting uneasy, too. My 'lesson' today didn't go well. I still don't know what they expect me to do, but I wasn't doing it. The man was ready to walk out mad."

"So you've noticed that too," said Peter. "I don't like it. You know what worries me? Suppose they decide that we can't be taught whatever they're trying to teach us? What then? Do we get put to sleep too?"

Lars shivered. "Hadn't thought of that."

Peter sat up on the edge of his bed. "I've thought of it plenty. I've also been thinking that there's more than one way to get through a brick wall. If you can't climb it, or dig under it, you can try smashing a hole in it." He jumped up, rubbing his hands together, sat down again for a moment, then stood up and went to the window. "I tell you, we've got to do something besides sit here! I don't care what, take a knife to one of them, or something, just to do *something*."

"You'd never get away with it. They'd spot you in a minute."

"Yes, that's just it! Everything we do or think, they know about. All they have to do is dip into our skulls and they know everything that's going on in there. But I think maybe their guard is down a little. They don't watch us so much now, and I've noticed that nobody pays much attention to us when we move around. Nobody has done any probing for days except during the lessons."

Lars nodded slowly. "That's true. So what?"

"So suppose we move fast and quietly and try to get out of here."

"Where to? Over the hills? They'd have us back the minute they missed us."

"Not if we had a Koenig drive pushing us, they wouldn't."

Lars stared. "You mean steal a ship?"

"Better than that." A flush of excitement rose in Peter's cheeks. "Look. We know where the men are sleeping. Suppose we went down there and woke them up. Not all of them, just enough to man a ship. If we could somehow keep our minds blank enough so that nobody would pick us up beforehand, we might be able to make a break for the *Ganymede* and get her aloft before they could stop us." He regarded Lars with a grin. "We wouldn't have to be very far out to throw in the drive. And once home, we could come back here with an armada if necessary."

"Suppose we can't wake them," said Lars bluntly. "They must be drugged."

"The City-people wake them enough to feed them, so they can't be too far under. And we know the City-people don't know enough to have put the ships out of commission."

Both boys were sitting on the edges of their beds now, wide awake, as the plan developed. They talked for an hour, checking every possible angle. At last Lars shook his head. "It's risky. If they nail us, they'll put us to sleep so fast we won't know what hit us."

"But they sleep, don't they? There won't be many awake at this hour, and why should they bother us if we keep our minds on some innocuous thought like going for a walk, or Mother Goose rhymes, or something? For that matter, if somebody does stop us, we can tell him that the Masters ordered us to do it! That'll slow them up for a while at least, maybe long enough for us to get away with it!"

Something flickered deep in Lars' mind then, and he frowned. It was as if a tiny set of gears had suddenly meshed. "Suppose these Masters *are* here in the city, after all," he said slowly. "Suppose the City-people are in contact with them all the time, conferring with them?"

"I don't think so. If they were, we'd have heard about it. They keep insisting that the Masters are gone."

"But if there *were* a place where the Masters could be contacted."

"Look, we could sit here and dream up all sorts of things, but it's not going to get us out of here," Peter cried. "I don't think we've got much longer. I think we're going to be sleeping like the rest of the crew, maybe forever, if we don't so something and do it now!"

"All right." Lars jumped to his feet, pulled his belt tight around the gray cloak that hung from his shoulders. "They're going to be a surprised bunch of people, I think."

"If we get away with it," added Peter.

"If we get away with it. Let's go."

Like shadows they moved through the door and down the darkened corridor toward the street.

14

THE DOOR BETWEEN

THE CITY was silent as a tomb. The glowing buildings had dimmed; the continual throb of mental activity that was always present in the bottom of Lars' mind was quiet, the barest whisper to witness that people were indeed alive here.

They moved along silent passages, carefully trying to marshal their thoughts along innocent lines, trying to keep out of their consciousness where they were going, or what they intended to do there. It was impossible to do completely but they tried, and they moved undisturbed down through level upon level of the city toward the vault.

They passed an old man in a corridor who looked at them with curiosity, but passed on. A group of young people were gathered at an intersection of arches, but they were so involved in their own thoughts they hardly noticed Lars and Peter as they passed quietly by.

They paused at the head of the staircase that led down to the vault. "If there's a guard, try to draw his attention without exciting him," Peter said in a whisper. "Then I'll try to jump him before he can give an alarm."

"Which ones are we going to waken?" Lars whispered back.

"Fox, for one, and Morehouse. Lambert and Lorry, if we have the chance. Ready now? Let's go."

They moved quickly down the stairs. In the great vault room they saw nobody except the rows of men sleeping on the pallets. And yet, as he blinked in the dim light, Lars had a fierce pang of misgiving. It was not right, doing it this way. Even if they succeeded, it meant leaving behind an alien people, the first contact with an alien race that Man had ever known. It meant leaving without understanding anything about these people, running out before the puzzle was solved. And worse, it would be the last chance to contact these strange City-people, for if Earthmen came back to Wolf IV, they would come as enemies.

What would Walter Fox do? The thought was strong in Lars' mind. He looked down the row of beds, saw the Commander's face placid now in sleep, and he seemed to hear his words: *Don't spoil it for us, Lars. Trust them. Offer them friendship. This is no time for hate or fear or mistrust.*

And now, without the least doubt, Lars knew what Fox would do. *There is a purpose here for the things that have come about, a reason, a solution to all the strange things that have happened since the* Ganymede *left Earth in search of the* Planetfall. *A link is missing, a key is waiting to fit the lock, if you can only find it. There is an answer.*

He hesitated, staring down at the rows of sleeping men as if he were in a dream himself.

Find the answer while you still can!

He turned to find Peter staring at him in alarm. "Lars! *I heard that,"* he whispered hoarsely.

"You—what?"

"I heard what you were thinking just then," Peter's face was white. "It was clear as crystal, as clear as if—they—had been thinking it."

Lars was trembling. "It's no good, Peter. We just can't do it this way."

"We can't go back now. We've got to try!"

"No, no. There's something else we have to try first. Like you said, you heard me thinking just then. You heard me before. And I've been picking things up from you, just snatches, here and there, but I have. Don't you see what that means?"

"I can see that we're going to be caught cold unless we move fast."

"That is what the lessons have been for, Peter. That is what the City-people have been trying to teach us. Only they didn't mean 'teach' the way we think of it, with book tapes and experimental labs. They haven't been teaching us, *they've been training us!"*

Peter stood stock-still. "'The Masters who fed us *and trained us,'"* he breathed.

"Of course! Trained them for what? Look around you at this city, man."

From all around them a wash of thought-patterns had been rising like a wave, alarmed, fearful, angry. They realized that they had almost been shouting at each other, and now Peter gave a groan of dismay as figures appeared at the end of the vault, on the stairs. "Too late!" he cried. "Run for it, Lars!"

But they couldn't run. The first of the City-people to see them gave a powerful cry of alarm, and they stood rooted unable to move, as more and more City-people tumbled down the stairs, eyes wide, staring at the boys and at the sleeping figures, a jumble of thoughts rushing from their minds.

The strangers, down here!

A forbidden place! What are they doing here?

They were going to waken the sleeping ones— And fear rose in a bubbling torrent as they stared at the boys in horror.

And then the woman who had been training Lars was coming through the group, her eyes angry, all trace of gentleness gone from her face. *We should never have waited for so long! We were wrong, it was hopeless from the start. And now even they would destroy us.*

Lars faced her, his eyes blazing. *You're wrong. We would not destroy you, or harm you.*

You came to waken these who sleep here. It was not accusation; she knew it was true, and thrust it at him as a fact.

Yes, we did but only when the Masters permit it.

The woman paused, as though he had caught her off guard. *But how could you know that the Masters permit it? The Masters said only when the time was ripe.*

Then now is the time. Lars felt his pulse pounding in his throat as he forced the thought into the woman's mind.

Now? So soon?

Lars' eyes were bright. *Now! There is a place of the Masters here, isn't that so?*

Yes, yes, of course.

Then we demand that you take us there. Now.

And then, suddenly, the City-people were crowding around them, eagerly. The fear was gone from their minds now; they were laughing and cheering as their eagerness overflowed in a powerful wave. From the woman the thought came directly to Lars: *If you demand it, we must do it. The Masters are no longer here, but there is a place here where they once were. We will take you there, if you are sure you are ready to go.*

It was an alien place.

The eerie, intangible alienness of it struck them both as they walked across the platform toward the oval black door before them.

It was like no other place in the city. The city and its strange people had been mysterious, puzzling, often inexplicable, different, but not *alien*. The things they had seen in the city at least showed some shadow of human thinking, of human minds at work.

But no human hands had built this place. Lars knew that as certainly as he knew his own name. It sat on a large circular platform, a building, if you could call it that, like a highly polished hemisphere with an oval black door in one side. Lars glanced helplessly at Peter by his side. "Have you ever seen this place before?"

"Never," Peter said. "And I don't like it."

"This is where the Masters are," Lars said. "This is where we'll find our answers."

"I hope so," said Peter, but his voice sounded as uncertain as Lars felt.

The woman had not led them here at once. First they had been taken back to their quarters, where a meal was waiting if they had been able to eat it. Fresh clothing was laid out, a hot running shower.

"Why, this is like a hanging in the old days back home!" Peter had cried out in dismay. "The last meal, the fancy preparations. You don't know what you've gotten us into!"

"But this is the answer we've been looking for, can't you see that?" Lars said. "I told you there would be a place where these Masters would be found, and there is!"

"What do you know about the Masters?" Peter's voice was bitter.

"No more than you do, but didn't you see how the people acted? Didn't you feel the—the *expectancy?* Peter, this is something we've been expected to do ever since we were brought into the city. This is what was *supposed to happen —sometime*."

"I think you're crazy," snapped Peter. "We haven't learned a thing that makes sense since we got here."

"But we can make some pretty good guesses," Lars said. "The ship on the ridge, for instance. It came here, some time a long time ago, and crashed. Now we know that it was a ship from Earth, the old *Argonaut*, carrying Earthmen. Not the ones that were aboard when it left Earth, of course, but those that were born en route. Right?"

"All right. So what?"

"The ship came, and crashed, and now, centuries later, another ship comes from Earth and finds a city on this planet with people living here. Very peculiar people, a very strange city, but *people*. It isn't coincidence, Peter. It can't be. These City-people are Earthmen. Their ancestors were born on Earth, just as certainly as yours were. Their fathers and grandfathers came here on the *Argonaut* and somehow came through the crash alive, and survived."

"But do you think they *act* like Earthmen?" Peter protested. "Building a city like this, using the powers they have—"

"Why not?" said Lars. "We know of these powers on Earth. They're pretty crude, but even the most stick-in-the-mud scientists recognize that they exist now: telepathy, telekinesis, teleportation. We knew about those things back in the twentieth century! Some workers in the field even claim that *all* Earthmen have those powers, to some very slight extent."

Lars changed into fresh clothing as Peter stared at him glumly. "But here we see people with extra-sensory powers magnified a thousand times, so strong their whole civilization is based on ESP. No wonder they don't know about science or mechanics. They don't need to. These people not only have ESP, *they know how to use it.*"

Peter chewed his lip. "And you think that the Masters, whatever they are, were the ones that trained them to use these powers?"

"Exactly. Just the way the City-people have been training us!"

"Then why just *us?* Why not the rest of the crewmen?"

"I don't know," said Lars, "but I think we're going to find out in this place they're taking us to."

It had seemed logical enough then, in the familiar surroundings of their room in the city, but now, facing the black oval doors Lars was no longer so certain. The City-people hung back at the edge of the platform, watching them expectantly as they approached the great hemisphere. At a distance the black oval looked like a yawning hole in the side of the thing, waiting to receive them. Only now they saw that it was a solid door, closed and fit so tightly that only a hairline crack showed around it. There was no knob, no handle. Nothing but polished black.

Lars and Peter stopped, and looked at each other. They felt the tension rising among the City-people behind them. "What do we do now?" Peter hissed. "This thing looks solid."

Lars reached out, pushed at the edge of the door. It didn't budge. "It *is* solid," he muttered.

"But we can't stop now. We've got to get in there."

"I think maybe we can," said Lars. "The lessons. The thing the City-people have been trying to train us to do. Maybe that's the key we need. Maybe we aren't supposed to get through this door until that training is completed."

"You mean teleportation," Peter said.

"*They* can do it," said Lars. He stared steadily at the heavy black slab, and suddenly imagined that once again he was staring at the viewscreen outside their quarters. He imagined that the woman from the city was there at his side, urging him on, guiding his mind. He tried to blot out all other thoughts, to concentrate every ounce of his strength on one single purpose:

To reach the other side of that door

He felt the sickening feeling grow in the pit of his stomach; then he felt himself jerk. Then, as though a light had been snapped off, he was through the door. He had not moved a muscle, but he was through it. An instant later Peter appeared by his side—out of nowhere.

The last barrier was behind them. They were in the place of the Masters.

At first Lars thought they were standing in the corridor outside their quarters in the city. He was inside, in semi-darkness, and his eyes picked up only the vague form of viewscreens for a moment. Then he accommodated, and saw other details.

The feeling of alienness remained. The chamber was hemispherical and almost bare, except for two viewscreens and two stools. By each viewscreen was a spindle filled with the flat, disc-like tape spools.

There was nothing else in the chamber. Lars glanced at Peter. *Then there are no Masters here,* he thought.

Peter nodded toward the screens. *No, but these tapes*

were left for us. Together they took places in front of the screens, and fed the tapes onto the reels.

The first ones were ordinary 3-V tapes. They were poor films, ancient and scratchy, very much like the home 3-V films Lars had often made years before. The images were poor, but they could make them out clearly.

They saw a Star Ship in its berth deep in the green mountain slopes. They saw cranes carrying up cargo, passengers. There was no question which ship it was. The ancient *Argonaut,* preparing for the Long Passage to Alpha Centauri.

The tape clicked, and they were looking through the after-ports, watching the billowing gust of blast-off, watching Earth dwindle and grow small behind. And through the forward ports, only the blackness of space. The crew of the *Argonaut* knew that they would never reach their destination; they would not live that long. But their children. . . .

There were many scenes and fragments on the view-screen then, films collected and stored by the crew of the Earth ship, an attempt to keep a history of the passage. Slowly the picture developed for Lars and Peter, a picture of bravery and frustration and failure.

The discovery that the course was wrong, that even the finest instruments in the finest laboratories on Earth had not been able to calculate and chart a course accurate enough for such a journey. Alpha Centauri approached, and passed, and dwindled in the distance as men died and babies were born. Not enough fuel to make the correction and hope for a safe landing. Nothing to do but plunge on toward something beyond, a faint star listed on the charts as Wolf.

Decades later the star-shapes had changed, and the destination star Wolf was near.

Finally, the approach to the star. A different crew, poorly trained, without adequate fuel, attempting to land the great ship on an alien planet—

Abruptly the tape flickered off.

Lars and Peter rested before the next tape. "They couldn't have landed it safely," Peter said slowly. "They must have known that, long before they tried it."

"Maybe," said Lars. "But their babies, I remember reading about the cradles that were installed on the *Argonaut*. To protect the new babies from almost any disaster." He filed the new tape on the spindle. "Perhaps there is more here."

The tapes were different now. Before, they had been records made by humans, seen through human eyes. Now it was different. There were no clear images on the viewscreen, yet Lars could see the images projected in his mind with perfect clarity. He realized, suddenly, that he was seeing through an alien mind, with alien thoughts, as the images flickered and changed.

An image of the Star Ship approaching, too fast, too hard, out of control. It came in shallow to the surface of Wolf IV, striking the high mountain ridge, driving down among the rocky crags, turning over in horrible slow motion as flame spurted up.

But not everyone aboard was dead. The crewmen, yes. But deep in the heart of the ship, the cradles nestled the children of the crewmen in strong steel arms, safe.

Alien creatures on the surface of Wolf IV saw the crash, searched the wreckage, hoping to learn something of the creatures who had come from so far. They found the records—tapes, films, voices, the library of the ship, the records of the crew and its history. Alien minds pored over them, learning, studying, seeking to see Earthmen as Earthmen had been on Earth.

But most of all they sought for signs that Earthmen had what they knew as the Strength, the universal power of mind that bound intelligent creatures throughout the universe into a union of peace and strength, and raised them above the beasts.

The alien creatures found only disappointment.

No trace of the Strength?

No trace. They were a barren race, to judge from their records. Vocal communication. Physical science and mechanical civilization. No evidence of the Strength anywhere. No sign that they could even recognize it.

But for a race to reach space without it—incredible!

You see it here.

Yes. Bitter disappointment. *Yes, we see it here.*

Then they found the cradles.

The spark of the Strength was there. Excited and eager, the alien creatures tore their way through bulkhead and deck, following the spark until they found the infants. The spark was feeble, barely perceptible, but it was there.

The records were sporadic then, as Lars and Peter sat by the viewscreens. It took months and years of teaching and training for the alien creatures to nurse the spark of Strength in those Earthling babies into a flame.

It could not have grown strong by itself. In Earthmen it was not a full-blown power but only a potential. It was weak. It had to be trained. As Earthmen on Earth grew from childhood into manhood, the unused potential faded until it was unrecoverable. To Earthmen, untrained, the spark of the Strength brought only confusion and pain, so it was buried deep in his mind, and lost, because he never suspected what it was or how to use it.

But the infants from the Star Ship were trained. They grew and developed as no human children ever had. There was nothing to quench the strong, cool flame in their minds, and it grew.

Their Strength, the extra-sensory powers of their heritage, grew strong as they grew.

When the work was done, the alien creatures left Wolf IV. The city was built, the City-people were safe, but there was still danger. If Earthmen were to come, without knowing of the Strength, they might destroy the aliens' work. Fear and hatred could cripple the City-people. The aliens knew this, and taught the City-people what to do. There could be no contact with Earth, not now. Some day contact could be made, but only when Earthmen from Earth could be taught to use their Strength as the City-people could.

Sometime an Earthman would come to Wolf IV, an Earthman old enough to understand Earthmen, and the minds of Earthmen, but still young enough for his Strength to be trained.

Only then could the gulf between the City-people and the men of Earth once more be bridged.

They finished the tapes, and stared at each other, and sat in silence for a long time. Then Lars felt a flicker of thought in his mind.

Lars? Can you hear me?

Yes. Perfectly.

Did you understand it, Lars? We're the ones. We of all the crew were still young enough to be trained.

Yes. And old enough to cross the gulf. We can make Earthmen understand what the Strength is and how to use it. Is that right? Is that what we have to do?

There was no hesitation in Peter's reply. *Yes. That's what we have to do.*

15

THE SLEEPERS AWAKE

COMMANDER WALTER Fox waited, stamping the floor impatiently as he stared through the window at the city below. The City-people had taken good care of their charges. The Commander's cheeks and arms had filled out somewhat, and the tired lines around his eyes were softer now. He felt the difference, and knew, somehow, that what had seemed like a moment's deep, dreamless sleep had been far longer than a moment.

Already the other men were being awakened, the remainder of his crew, and the ones from the *Planetfall* who had slept so long. Commander Fox did not know what had happened, but the City-people had been kind. There had been no sign of hostility. Indeed, they had seemed overjoyed as they crowded around to see the sleepers walking up from the vault, as though a great day had somehow arrived in their lives.

Presently a tall man from the city came to him and led him across the archway, into the silvery ship lying on the ramp—his own ship, the *Ganymede*. He found Lars and Peter waiting in the control room, and clasped their hands tightly. "You made contact, then," he said.

"Yes. Contact was made. But these people are not the aliens. They're Earthmen like us but with a very great difference."

Carefully, with all the details, they told him of the Place of the Masters and what they had found there. They told him of their period of training with the City-people. They told him of the Strength and what it meant to mankind that these children of the *Argonaut* had developed it.

The Commander listened silently as the story unfolded. At last he said, "Then this Strength is extra-sensory power."

"Magnified a thousand times from what we know it," said Lars. "It is a staggering power, so great it puts the Koenig drive in the kindergarten class. But it isn't the things that it can *do* that count so much. It means men can understand each other completely. It means they can move with complete freedom, accomplish things they have never dreamed of. Remember that these City-people have been limited by isolation. Wait until they have been taught of the universe around them, of Earth, and the stars!"

"And Earthmen can be like that?"

"Every Earthman has some vestige of the Strength. The young ones can still be trained. That's our job. To show Earthmen what they have had in their grasp all these centuries and never seen."

Fox nodded slowly. "And the aliens?"

"The Masters were aliens."

"You never actually confronted them, then."

Lars shrugged. "Yes and no. They left Wolf IV when their work here was done This was not their native home. But they left something else behind."

Lars unfolded the chart, a glimmering metallic thing that glowed with star-dots. "This will tell us where they came from and to where they returned. Sometime we will confront them, if we want to. But we know already the most important thing—that they are *good*. We need never fear aliens again. They have shown us the potential we have if we want to learn to use it."

"And now?"

"We have to learn to use it, of course," said Peter, who had been sitting silent. "We have to go home. Ambassadors, you might say, Lars and I."

Fox nodded again, trying to absorb the things they were saying. "But the others—the deserters—"

"Does it matter about the deserters?" Peter said. "The *Ganymede* has completed her mission. Does anything else matter?"

Fox was hesitant. "A clean slate, then?"

"Why not? Salter can't hurt anybody now."

"All right. A clean slate."

The ship rose slowly, leaving the gray ragged surface of the planet far behind. No fire from its jets. No roar from its motors. A greater power lifted it like a feather, until distance allowed the Koenig drive to be started. Behind the *Ganymede* the *Planetfall* rose also. Together they flickered and vanished into the envelope of power that would carry them home. They had reached Limbo, and survived.

And now, returning, they carried a new heritage for Earthmen. There would be many ships, and many men, before they learned to use the Strength, but they would learn it.

They knew now that a universe was waiting for them.